THE MAN OF BRONZE

Doc Savage travels the globe, righting wrongs, helping the oppressed, giving good guys the break, and punishing evildoers, but never taking a life if there's any way out. Doc's "college," for instance, is a scientific institution in upper New York where he sends all captured crooks. Through expert treatment and sometimes involved operations—for Doc Savage is one of the world's most skilled surgeons—they are made to forget their past and start life anew as useful and decent citizens.

Bantam Books by Kenneth Robeson
Ask your bookseller for the books you have missed

About Doc Savage®
     DOC SAVAGE: HIS APOCALYPTIC LIFE
     by Philip José Farmer

THE
FLYING GOBLIN

A DOC SAVAGE® ADVENTURE

by Kenneth Robeson

BANTAM BOOKS
TORONTO · NEW YORK · LONDON

THE FLYING GOBLIN

*A Bantam Book / published by arrangement with
The Condé Nast Publications Inc.*

PRINTING HISTORY
Originally published in DOC SAVAGE *Magazine July 1940*
Bantam edition / September 1977

ISBN 0-553-11190-6

Published simultaneously in the United States and Canada

---

*Bantam Books are published by Bantam Books, Inc. Its trade-
mark, consisting of the words "Bantam Books" and the por-
trayal of a bantam, is registered in the United States Patent
Office and in other countries. Marca Registrada. Bantam
Books, Inc., 666 Fifth Avenue, New York, New York 10019.*

PRINTED IN THE UNITED STATES OF AMERICA

CONTENTS

Chapter I

BIRMINGHAM JONES

The long, many-windowed building was located in almost primeval wilderness. The somber-looking mountains of upstate New York rose around it, gauntlike in the night gloom. The building looked like a modern city institution transplanted to a quiet spot, where, especially at this hour of the night, nothing could possibly ever happen.

There were the soft night sounds of little animals in the surrounding woods. A solitary dim light burned in what was perhaps an office of the hospital-type edifice. There was deep silence, an air of calmness everywhere. A rabbit scurried silently across the single dusty road that wound up to the place.

It looked as though nothing of importance could ever happen in such a wilderness setting.

But because a man named Birmingham Jones was housed within the walls of the building, a whole lot of trouble was going to take place. At least, this seemed to be the opinion of the two shadowy men who crouched in deep shrubs bordering a flat expanse of smooth lawn behind the building.

Both men wore clothes that looked as though they had been ripped and frayed by passing through assorted thorns and brush. Both had faces that might have been bruised in the same manner—only the scars were old and had been collected over a long period of years, obviously.

Both kept watching the walls of the building that loomed so close to them. Windows in those straight walls were barred with heavy iron.

One man whispered to his partner, "It's the fourth window from the left-hand wall angle. Third floor."

"You're sure about that, Pinky?"

"Damn right. You ever hear of the boss making mistakes?"

Apparently the other had not. "No, but I wanna make sure *you're* correct. Hell, if we ever make a mistake—"

"There ain't no mistake about this," said the one named Pinky. "Here."

He passed his hard-looking partner something white, wrapped around a stone. He motioned to the window not far away.

"The boss," Pinky said, "picked you for this job special, because you've thrown enough bombs in your day to be good. That note's got to land in Birmingham's room. The lower sash is raised. See it? Now, get going!"

The other paused a moment.

"Look, you sure this note tells Birmingham Jones everything he's to do?"

Pinky nodded impatiently. "Yeah, sure. In five minutes, he gets out. He gets sprung. Right through that building corner that ain't gonna be any more!"

Both men, at the words, consulted their watches. "Four minutes and a half," snapped Pinky worriedly. "You better hurry."

His partner drifted silently toward the base of the building wall. A dozen feet away, he took careful aim, threw the paper-wrapped missile in an overhand swing.

The object passed neatly between the iron bars of the window that Pinky had shortly before indicated. From the room beyond, there was the faintest of thumps audible out here in the peaceful, warm night.

The man faded back toward the bushes where Pinky was waiting.

"Look!" Pinky said suddenly.

Both men saw the brief wave of a hand from the second-floor room. They turned and ducked beneath the enshrouding trees. A half moment later they reached the dusty, narrow roadway and took out for points distant as though the very devil were after them.

And three and a half moments later, the devil did seem to appear.

First, there was the peculiar whining sound, like wind blowing through guide wires on a towering wireless-station antenna.

The hobgoblin of a thing that followed the whining sound streaked down out of the night sky with the wild speed of a diving pursuit plane. Only no plane had ever traveled as fast as the peculiar-shaped object.

It might have been a long, lean barrel. Astride it was a vague form that appeared like a scarecrow with flapping arms.

One moment the flying apparition was a quarter of a mile away. The next it clipped the corner of the building wall that had been indicated by Pinky.

It sounded as though a part of the war in Europe had suddenly been moved to the wilderness of upstate New York. At least, that's the noise the flying thing made as it struck the building corner. That part of the place started falling down.

Far down the dusty road, from where their car was protected and concealed beneath low-hanging trees, Pinky grabbed the thick arm of his partner and grinned. He looked happy at the sound of the explosions that were coming from back up the road.

"Right on the nose," he remarked, consulting his watch. "The boss sure don't miss on timing."

His partner looked less confident. "Maybe that thing killed Birmingham!"

Pinky shook his head. "Naw. Bet you he'll be along in a couple minutes—*if* he reads that message right."

His thickset partner gave him a questioning look. "You mean Birmingham's still foggy?"

Pinky nodded.

"That tricky brain operation which that Doc Savage guy uses on crooks at his college didn't quite come off in Birmingham's case. Sure, he's forgotten all about what he ever did in the past; but that's all. We're springing him right at a time when he'll make a swell front for the boss. I understand he's just like a trained seal. He'll do anything you tell him—and no questions asked."

Both men had climbed out of the car and were now watching back down the seldom-used road.

"But," objected Pinky's partner, "I understood that when Doc Savage got through with these patients of his that they stopped being crooks?"

Pinky laughed harshly.

"Sure, they do. But they weren't through with Birmingham Jones yet. And there's something else."

"Else?"

Pinky nodded. "Birmingham got conked on the head by one of Dillinger's boys some years back. Seems, therefore, this Doc Savage outfit couldn't quite cure Birmingham of being a crook. Also, he still likes to kill people. That's how Doc Savage first happened to send him up to his college."

The other man whistled.

The "college" referred to was an institution established by Doc Savage—known as the Man of Bronze —where crooks caught by the bronze man and his aids were sent to undergo delicate brain operations devised by Doc Savage himself.

The operations, in most cases, wiped out all memories of the patients' past. They were then fitted for worth-while work in a social world that would again accept them.

But in the case of Birmingham Jones, apparently,

only about half of the experiment had been successful, according to Pinky's remarks.

He started to say, "If everything's gone O. K., Birmingham Jones should be—"

He clamped his jaw shut, stared narrowly at the tall, well-dressed man who stepped out of the woods almost directly in his path.

Both Pinky and his partner went for their shoulder holsters.

And both paused, gawking at the automatic which appeared miraculously—and swiftly—in the hands of the tall, dark-haired man.

The stranger had smooth features, a fairly large mouth and eyes that were gray. They were peculiar eyes. Peculiar in the fact that, when you met their unblinking regard, you felt a funny feeling along your spine.

"I like to kill people," said the stranger. "I get a kick out of it. I'd just as well kill you two punks. But the note said you were to take me to Valentine."

Pinky gulped. His partner jumped.

"Gosh blazes!" said Pinky. "Are *you* Birmingham Jones?"

The tall, dark man's features showed no expression. "So they inform me," he said. "And the note that came through the window was addressed to me. So I escaped when the explosion came. I was to come here. Where's this guy Valentine?"

Pinky was suddenly gripping the tall man's arm, hurrying him toward the car.

"Brother," he said happily, "for a guy who forgets all about the past, you sure follow orders nicely! You're gonna get along with Valentine O. K."

Birmingham Jones put his automatic away, climbed into the back seat of the waiting sedan and remarked, "Who's Valentine?"

Pinky sighed, pausing in his movement at climbing behind the wheel of the car.

"Look," he explained, "you got the first letter we smuggled into that college to you?"

Tall Birmingham Jones nodded.

"And you want to work for a guy who's got plenty of chips?"

"Naturally."

"Well, Valentine's the gent who's arranged all this for you. You can be a big shot now. You're gonna be bigger than Pretty Boy Floyd, or Scarface Nelson, or—"

Pinky had finally started up, his partner seated beside him.

"Who were they?" asked Birmingham Jones.

Pinky swallowed hard. "Hell!" he gasped. "You rubbed out about three guys when you were a member of one of them mobs!"

"How nice," remarked Birmingham casually. "Who do I rub out now?"

Pinky nudged his partner, whispering beneath the motor hum of the moving car, "Foggy. He's still foggy."

And to the man in the rear seat, in a loud voice. "Brother, maybe there'll be plenty for you to take care of. The boss has a lot on the fire. Big stuff. He—"

Pinky turned around a second, frowned when he saw that Birmingham Jones was not apparently listening. Instead, the well-dressed man was grinning about something as he examined the gun which he again held in his hands.

"What you smiling about?" Pinky asked cautiously.

"I was just thinking about that explosion back there at the college. It was good. Three guards were still under the smashed brick wall when I walked out. I got this gat from one of them."

He put the gun away again, asked, "Well, what's my first job? What does this Valentine want me to do first?"

The grin returned to Pinky's hard face.

"Birmingham," he said, "it's a swell assignment. First, you gotta grab the girl."

"What girl?"

"The girl that saw Oscar."

"Oscar who?"

Pinky laughed hard. "Oscar's the fellow who helped you get out of the college, brother." His face sobered again. "And this girl, this Honey Sanders, she saw Oscar. Also, the boss figures maybe she got some clue to *him*. So now you gotta grab this person named Honey Sanders."

"Where?"

"Down near New York, a place called Sleepy Hollow. That's where that Ichabod Crane, the headless horseman, used to hang out. Remember him?"

Birmingham Jones shook his head. "Never heard of him," he remarked absently. "Thought they gave them the chair in New York State. How'd the guy lose his head?"

Pinky howled, almost doubling up with laughter over the steering wheel.

"Maybe," he said finally, "Honey Sanders can answer that one for you."

Chapter II

GOBLIN IN SLEEPY HOLLOW

Approximately two hundred miles south of where Birmingham Jones was riding with his two rescuers, two other men were driving in an open car. It was fifteen minutes past midnight, just a quarter of an hour since the strange explosion had taken place at the "college" of Doc Savage, upstate.

Neither of these two, naturally, knew about the weird occurrence at Doc Savage's institution. But they did seem to know something about a girl named Honey Sanders.

The man who was not driving—a lean-waisted, nattily dressed fellow with fairly good-looking features

—held a newspaper spread across his knees. He was reading the paper by aid of the dashboard light in the roadster.

"It says," he said, "that this girl Honey Sanders lives here in Sleepy Hollow Manor, near Tarrytown. And the guy back there at the last gas station informed us to take the first left turn-off from the Post Road. So this must be right."

"If it is, I still won't believe it!" said the one behind the wheel. "Just because you said so, I won't believe it!"

The speaker had shoulders half the width of the car seat, a flat head that squatted, seemingly, right atop those shoulders, and a scarred face made to frighten old ladies. Oddly, he looked like an ape; an ape in a human's clothing.

The fashionably dressed man kept addressing him as Monk.

"Listen," the one named Monk added, "read them headlines over again. If you've made a mistake, I'm gonna whack you so hard on the head that you'll have these cushion springs for curls."

The dapper-looking man with the paper on his knees merely glared at the driver. Then he started reading from the headlines. He said:

"This Honey Sanders, it appears, saw the apparition last night, here in Sleepy Hollow. She was walking down near the river when something passed over her head. As she told reporters, the only thing she could think of was the headless horseman—that guy made famous in Irving's 'Legend of Sleepy Hollow.'"

Monk squinted at his companion. "You mean that Ichabod What's-his-name?"

"Ichabod Crane, you dope!" snapped the well-dressed man.

"And so?" prodded Monk, the driver of the car.

"It seems she was frightened terribly as she told reporters about the strange thing flying through the air. And now, today, the paper goes on to say that she has mysteriously disappeared."

Monk snorted. "Look, Ham, you shyster, I already

know all that. What I wanna know is: What was that address of Honey Sanders? You sure this is the right place?"

The man called Ham sighed.

"Yes," he said crisply. "It's right here—Shady Lane, in Sleepy Hollow Manor. And this is the right road. It's supposed to be a little cottage down at the end of this winding lane."

Ham settled back, watching the shaded lane the car was traversing. They had passed no houses since leaving the well-traveled Post Road.

The lane dropped down through a hollow damp with the nearness of a stagnant-looking pond. A bullfrog croaked somewhere out on the water. Thick silence otherwise pressed down over the lonely spot.

Hairy Monk asked, "This where that headless horseman guy used to hang out?"

Ham nodded. "Yes. This is Sleepy Hollow."

Swinging abruptly away from the wheel, disregarding the narrow roadway ahead, Monk started to say something. "Blazes—"

But he broke off, his little eyes jerking to the sky overhead. The car stalled as Monk's foot smashed down on the brake.

From out of the night sky, a weird, thin whining sound had come. It increased swiftly, developing within seconds into a keening shrill whistle that hurt the eardrums.

Monk, staring out of popping eyes, demanded loudly, "Gosh-amighty, *what was that?*"

In the next second, something ripped furiously through the trees overhead. A breeze swooped down and fanned the two men's heads. Loosened leaves cascaded around them like falling snow during a blizzard. The shrill whining sound faded.

Monk and Ham were both staring, wide-eyed, at the great swath cut through the tops of the trees. It was as though a giant scythe might have neatly cut a pathway a yard wide through the treetops.

Somehow, Monk got the car started, slammed through the speeds, swung the machine around in the narrow roadway and headed, recklessly, back toward the Post Road which passed through nearby Tarrytown.

Ham, the well-dressed one, yelled above the motor roar, "What's wrong with you, ape?"

"Blasted spook, that's what it was!" Monk piped. "Didn't you see it?"

"See what?"

Monk's small eyes were centered on the winding road. He was sending the car hurtling along at close to sixty.

"The danged *hobgoblin* riding the barrel that shot through the trees!" Suddenly Monk's massive hand cracked down on the wheel and he let out a whoop. "That's who it was! Ichabod—the guy without a head. Saw him plain as day riding that thing through the sky!"

Ham was frowning. "Now listen—" he started, and got no further.

For at the tremendous speed at which they were traveling, they had quickly reached the main highway again. Without even letting up on the gas, Monk wheeled the car out onto the wide Post Road, cut south, opened up on the throttle.

Luckily at the moment and because of the hour, there was no traffic. A good mile stretch of open highway opened up before them. Monk was driving like a demon.

The weird whining sound came down out of the sky again.

Ham, clinging to his hat, rose halfway out of the seat and stared, goggle-eyed, into the heavens. The thing, which moved with the speed of a flashing comet, dropped down low over the racing car. Ham had a glimpse of something that looked like a long, thin barrel with a vague form sitting astride it.

Before he could study the uncanny-looking object closer, he threw himself low in the seat and yelled, *"Look out!"*

The thin whining sound was next a screech directly over their heads. There was something like a terrific blast of air, wind striking them with the force of a trimotored plane's slipstream.

Monk flung his hairy hands about his homely face. His companion reached for the door handle of the car.

Neither, apparently, remembered exactly how the car got piled up in the gas-station driveway.

But the station owner—who had been preparing to close up for the night—was jumping up and down and making noises, when Monk finally crawled out of the partially demolished machine.

Ham, unhurt, but his immaculate clothes mussed, followed.

The service-station owner was a long man in overalls. He was gesticulating wildly toward a gas pump. The pump looked like a candle that had stood in a warm room; it was leaning over at a cockeyed angle.

"Gah . . . ga . . ." the owner tried to get words out, and his face became crimson as he choked with rage. His hands grasped Monk's coat collar and yanked him clear of the wrecked car.

"Drunk!" the station owner finally exploded. "Look what you've done! Guys like you—"

The man got his first good look at Monk, who, so far, had been weaving around still in a daze.

Jerking his gaze to Ham, the man frowned and said, "He looks like something that's escaped from an organ grinder!"

Ham let out a howl at that.

"He did!" Ham announced. "Only he lost his tin cup in this smashup!"

The words must have penetrated Monk's dazed thoughts. He gave a snort of rage and grabbed the station owner by the neck.

"I'm gonna rattle your teeth loose for that crack!" he roared.

The gas-station owner broke free, leaped inside the small building and picked up a heavy wrench. Monk followed. Ham gave a worried cry and tried to separate the two.

When the State trooper on the motorcycle drove into the station driveway, some more wreckage had been created. Quart bottles of oil with spouts on them had been knocked from a rack and smashed. Monk and the tall station owner were smeared from head to foot with sticky, dark oil. Windows in the building were broken. Ham was attempting to help out—trying, at the same time, to avoid stepping into the slippery oil.

The six-foot-two trooper joined the mêlée.

Later, three police officers from the nearby town arrived. Even with their help, it was another fifteen minutes before Monk was finally subdued.

The subduing includes tying Monk up with ropes, wire and two skid chains found in the service station. Ham rode along as Monk was carried off to the local jail, a mile down the highway.

The place consisted of a large room that was a littered office, beyond this a smaller room at the rear of which were two barred cells. Monk was unbound and thrown into one of the cells. Ham was not locked up, but the three officers and the trooper looked at him suspiciously. They indicated a chair for Ham and they all sat down, outside the cells.

"What are we waiting for?" Ham demanded.

One of the local cops said, "Sandy Gower."

"Who is Sandy Gower?" Ham prodded.

"The constable."

Ham, watching Monk's homely, bruised face stuck between two of the cell bars, gave a broad grin. "This is going to be good," he remarked.

Monk, by this time, had cooled off somewhat. He said worriedly, "Listen, you chumps, I saw it, I tell you. I saw the danged thing right over my head!"

"Saw what?" one of the cops demanded.

"That gollywockus. That spook. Ichabod!"

The State trooper gave his law companions a significant look.

"Good thing we caught him in time," he said quietly.

Monk grasped the bars. "Blast it!" he said. "I'm telling you! It was flying right over my head, an' it had flapping arms and a long skinny body. The danged thing—"

The trooper spoke to one of the local officers. "You'd better call up Hudson State."

Monk banged his huge fists on the cell bars.

"What's that?" he demanded.

"The nuthouse!"

"Hey!" Monk squalled. "You blasted fools. If I don't get outa here—"

They were all interrupted by the short, stocky man who entered the outer office. Ham, in particular, gave a start.

The arrival wore a loud tweed suit. His hat was green. The necktie was exceptionally loud.

Ham, a meticulous dresser, shuddered at sight of the solid little man's clothes.

"That's Sandy Gower," offered the trooper.

The constable had short, stubby hair like pale straw-ends, little sharp eyes that were as gray as ice. As he stepped toward the call room, he paused at a battered desk, picked up an ash tray and brought it along with him.

He gave Ham a brief, quizzical look, then sat down in one of the chairs and carefully balanced the ash tray on his knees. He took a large pipe from his pocket, and next started splitting open the paper on cigarette butts that were in the ash tray. He packed the released tobacco into his pipe.

If he had noted Monk, behind the bars nearby, he paid no attention to the fact. It took Sandy Gower several minutes to get the pipe fixed. Then he looked up at Ham and asked:

"Got a match?"

Holding a light for the stocky little constable, Ham said, "Perhaps I should introduce myself. The name is Brigadier General Theodore Marley Brooks. I happen to be an attorney. Perhaps something can be done about—"

From the cell, Monk remarked, "An' he's still a ham!"

The constable, Sandy Gower, was apparently paying no attention. He was more interested in getting his pipe started.

Finally, he indicated Monk, took in Ham's mussed clothes, asked, "What goes on?"

Ham tried to explain about the accident at the gas station. He talked swiftly, convincingly, and—oddly—did not try to lay the blame on Monk.

As he said, "His name is Lieutenant Colonel Andrew Bodgett Mayfair, though for obvious reasons—we call him Monk. Believe it or not, he is a well-known chemist. If there's anything I can do for him—"

Sandy Gower stopped puffing on the evil-smelling pipe and frowned. His ruddy face wrinkled up.

"Nope!" he said flatly. "We'll have to hold him for a hearing before the judge in the morning."

Ham talked some more, using his best courtroom manner. For Ham was a Harvard graduate, a renowned scholar from the law school there. More than once he had swayed frozen-faced juries.

But as he talked, Sandy Gower kept shaking his head. "Nope," he repeated, taking a good look at Monk, behind the bars. "I ain't a-gonna do it." He stared at Monk. "That bird don't look human. Better keep him locked up."

Monk roared with rage. "Say, you danged over-dressed signboard!" he said to the stocky constable. "If Doc Savage—"

Sandy Gower jumped. He jerked around to stare at well-dressed Ham, and he forgot to puff on his pipe.

"Did that monkey say 'Doc Savage'?" he demanded.

Ham had not wanted to mention the bronze man's name. But now he nodded.

"Yes. We are both members of the organization of Doc Savage. As I was telling you about this accident—"

Sandy Gower looked as though he was about to swallow his pipe. Still staring at Ham, he said politely, "Well, hell, that's different! We will not have to hold you. I am very sorry you were put to this inconvenience."

He paused, turned again to stare questioningly at

Monk. "But I'm afraid I can do nothing—yet—about this one. That young man who runs the gas station is a personal friend. He phoned me just a little while ago, and he's going to sign a complaint against your partner. Otherwise—"

Ham smiled broadly. "Perhaps," he said, casting a sidelong grin at Monk, "it will do him good to cool off for the remainder of the night."

He started out, the solidly built constable with him. Behind them, Monk set up a roar of protest.

"Why, you blasted shyster—"

But outside, Ham was saying, "There's a girl named Honey Sanders for whom we've been looking. It seems—"

Sandy Gower drew up short outside the jail. "You know about *her?*" he exclaimed.

Ham mentioned the newspaper story about the girl who had apparently been frightened to death by some strange hobgoblin of a thing which she had seen in this vicinity.

The constable was puffing quite furiously on his pipe now. "Yes. Yes, I know," he said. "When last seen, Honey Sanders was hysterical. Then she disappeared, and we've been looking for her for the past twenty-four hours."

"Then you know her?"

Sandy Gower jerked his head. "I've known the poor child for some time. If there's anything I can do to help—"

He led the way toward an old flivver parked nearby.

"I'll show you where she lives," the loudly dressed constable offered.

Chapter III

THE SIX WHO KNEW OSCAR

The cottage was white, with blue shutters, and must have contained about three rooms.

Ham, studying it, thought it just about suited a girl with the name Honey. He was getting more and more anxious to meet the girl.

Ham and Sandy Gower, the hard-boiled constable, were standing in the pathway that led in from the road. Beyond the cottage, down below a steep enbankment, lay the Hudson River. In a cut at the bottom of the high bank there were the smooth rails of a railroad.

Sandy Gower was saying, "She lived alone down here. Her mother and father are dead. She paints."

"You've searched through the house?" Ham asked.

The stocky constable nodded. "There isn't a trace of Honey Sanders," he explained.

Ham was thinking quickly. He, too, would like to have a look inside the girl's neat little cottage. And yet he did not wish to involve Doc Savage in this thing —and that would be necessary if he gave this law official the idea that it was too urgent to see the girl.

For Doc Savage knew nothing about a girl named Honey Sanders. The bronze man had been away from New York when Monk and Ham had seen the newspaper article about the terrified girl. Out of idle curiosity, they had taken a run up here tonight.

So, on a sudden pretense, Ham exclaimed suddenly, "Gosh, I just remembered!"

Sandy Gower removed the pipe from his mouth. "Remembered what?"

"Monk—that fellow you still have in jail—and I were driving down this lane earlier. We didn't get quite this far, though. But at the time, when Monk got excited about seeing some sort of flying apparition, I dropped a small camera we had brought along. Maybe I can find it up the lane."

Ham indicated the curving roadway that emerged from the woods, near the cottage.

"But," he added worriedly, "I really ought to see that gas-station fellow first. About the damage we did there, and about our car. Perhaps he can repair it, or—"

Sandy Gower took the bait nicely.

"Look," he offered, "I'll be glad to run back there for you while you're looking around for that camera. If there's anything I can do—"

Ham gave his broadest smile. "Swell!" he said. "And here—"

He took a roll of bills from his pocket, removed several and handed them over to the constable. "Fix things up with the chap, will you? Tell him I'll pay extra for any work done on the car before morning. He can name his own price."

Sandy Gower nodded, pocketing the money and moving toward his dilapidated-looking car. Ham's smooth talk had convinced the lawman that he was doing a favor for someone of importance.

A moment after Sandy Gower's car chugged away down the lane, Ham was seeking entry to the girl's modest cottage. After trying several windows, he learned that entry to the place was simple. The rear door was unlocked.

Inside, he passed through a neat little kitchen done in white with red decorations. He passed on to the living room, using a small pocket flash to look over the interior of the house.

The living room was across a hallway from what was apparently a combination studio-and-sleeping room. There was more space than Ham had imagined from outside the small cottage.

He looked at paintings hanging from the walls, leaning against furniture. There was one on an easel. They were landscapes, and not bad at all.

Moonlight came out from behind a cloud over the house and sprayed into the studio room. Ham snapped off the flash. He was able to see without it, and it was best that he take no chances on anyone spotting him in the girl's home.

The full-length portrait that stood in a corner of the room wasn't bad, either. In fact, it was quite lovely.

Against the white background of the canvas, it showed a slender, daintily built girl with hair the color of honey and features that were smooth and fine. The eyes were done so well that Ham was certain they were deep blue.

He stood gazing at the painting, wondering if it was only in pictures that you saw a young girl as pretty as this. He moved forward to get a better view of the thing.

The image moved!

Ham gulped. He saw the small, efficient-looking gun that was covering him.

The girl's taut voice said, "If you come a step closer, I'll shoot you!"

It took five minutes of lawyer Ham's cleverest talking to convince the girl that he shouldn't be shot as a trespasser.

She was the girl he and Monk had been seeking —Honey Sanders.

Finally, she was convinced. Her nicely curved lower lip trembled slightly. The gun lowered in her hand and she stepped away from the easel that contained the large, blank canvas behind her. It was this that had given the painting effect as the girl stood before it. Ham had been correct; her eyes *were* the deepest blue.

Honey Sanders said, "I believe what you say. I've heard of Doc Savage. I've heard of you, too. You're the one who has leading tailors follow him around in order to observe the very latest in men's fashions."

Ham stammered something. Yet he was pleased.

"Then perhaps I can help you," Ham suggested. "What was this terrible thing you saw? What is it all about?"

"I don't know!" Honey Sanders announced surprisingly.

"You don't know?" Ham stared. "But—"

"What I mean is, I don't know what the flying thing is. But I can tell you this: It comes from some place out on the river. I'm certain of that."

Ham frowned. "But the newspaper reports stated that, when you were last seen, you were terrified about something."

Honey Sanders jerked her pretty head. "Yes. Because of the men."

"What men?"

The girl reached out a shapely hand, touched the smartly dressed lawyer's arm.

"If you'll come with me," she suggested, "I can show you where I first overheard the men talking. They were planning something—something tremendous. That's why I have been so terrified. I think they have some connection with that . . . that thing that flew over my house."

"But why—"

"You see," continued Honey Sanders, her blue eyes wide, "one of them followed me. I'm certain he was going to kill me. I've been hiding."

Ham followed the girl from the house, watched her lock the kitchen door. The route she indicated led down a path cutting through tall grass toward the river and the railroad tracks. The girl took the lead. Moonlight bathed her soft-gold hair, the smooth manner in which she walked.

Over her shoulder, Honey Sanders said, "There's something odd about a little building up here about a quarter of a mile, on the bank above the railroad tracks. I've tried to get into it, but it's locked up."

Ham asked: "What has that got to do with a man who followed you or with something you saw flying around Sleepy Hollow?"

It was a moment before the girl answered.

"Well," she finally said, "they seemed to be planning a meeting at this stone building when I overheard them. But I stepped on something in the dark, and one of them almost found me when I hid in the woods."

Ham made no comment.

So far, this whole business did not seem quite to mystify him as it had apparently affected others. Perhaps this girl Honey Sanders was working some publicity stunt just to get her name in the papers. Less attractive girls had pulled similar gags.

And yet there was the thing that Monk had described zooming through the night. True, Monk had plenty of imagination. Ham himself had looked just a second too late to be certain as to what, exactly, the thing *was*.

But there had been something, and it had left a small hurricane closing in behind it because of its tremendous speed.

The girl had paused. She took Ham's arm, said quietly, "There! Just ahead of us. That small stone building that looks like an old blockhouse. I'm certain those men were planning a meeting there!"

Ham moved quietly ahead, the girl close to his side, her head barely reaching to his shoulders.

They came up to the dark, drab-looking building. It was about twelve feet high and twice that many square. There were no windows, strangely. And no doors, either!

Ham shrugged. "Must be some old place left from the Revolution, and it's been cemented up," was his observation.

Honey Sanders pointed off toward the wide Hudson. "And out there, about in the middle of the river," she said, "was where that terrible flying thing disappeared the other night."

The tall lawyer followed the girl's slim, pointing finger.

Out on the calm water, a tug was towing barges upstream. There must have been five barges in tow, for Ham counted five white lights on a mast sticking up from the tugboat. He saw nothing else.

He looked back at Honey Sanders. She was a pretty

girl. She had a direct manner and frank, clear eyes. Thus he didn't want to believe what was in his mind.

And yet he was convinced suddenly, that he was getting some sort of runaround.

Ham started to say, "Now let's get this straight—"

"*Listen!*" the girl gasped, and clung to Ham's arm.

The faint humming was about as loud as the sound a bee makes.

A moment later, the sound had increased to a high, shrill whine.

Honey Sanders trembled with sudden terror, close to Ham. She gasped, "Th . . . that's it! That's the *thing!*"

The girl's fear-filled eyes were probing the sky overhead.

Clouds scudded past the moon. There were a few stars. Though he heard the increasing, weird whining, Ham saw nothing.

And then he did!

Not a cloud in front of the moon, but something that moved with flashing, deceiving speed. It seemed to leap into larger proportions in the very second he spotted it. But a drifting cloud as abruptly cut off sight of the strange object.

The whistling sound was almost a roar now in Ham's ears. With sudden concern, Ham was grabbing the girl's trim figure and pulling her down toward the ground. For he abruptly realized that he had been deceived. The flying object was almost on top of them!

Ham and the girl pressed close to the earth. A blast of driven air came down and flattened out the tall grass around them. Dust and small pebbles spattered their faces and hands. They were both momentarily deafened by the shrill screech above them.

Then the strange object had passed.

Ham was on his feet, as was the girl. She pointed excitedly toward the river again.

"You see!" she cried. "That's where it disappeared to the last time—out there on the river some place!"

Ham squinted into the night. Far across the river

there were enough small hills to cast shadows out upon the water on that side. Impossible to tell whether anything was there on the water close to the far shore.

He looked down across the railroad tracks, saw some small boats tied up at the nearby shore. "Come on!" he snapped.

A block-signal tower a little way up the tracks suddenly showed two green lights.

Ham said, "We'd better wait before crossing. A train's coming."

It was a long freight, and Ham cursed his luck as the seemingly endless line of cars rattled past. They waited all of five minutes until the caboose rolled into sight.

"All right," Ham said, taking the girl's hand as the last car was next to them.

They started across the four sets of rails.

The half-dozen gunmen stood facing them. They had been hidden by the passing freight.

Ham made an unconscious movement with his right arm, as though raising something. And, then he muttered a soft, "Damn!"

He was without his cane, remembering that it was back in the car at the gas station. And that cane sheathed a finely tempered steel blade that, more than once, had saved the astute lawyer's life. Its tip was treated with a quick-acting anaesthetic!

The six men with guns had by this time closed in around Ham and the girl.

One man growled, "All right. Get back up that path you just climbed down! Step on it!"

Honey Sanders was directed to go first. Ham followed. Just as they started up the steep incline of the embankment, the lawyer's hand darted beneath his coat and toward a shoulder holster. The gunmen were behind him.

But something smacked against the back of his head. He was knocked to his face. Three of the thugs leaped upon Ham and removed the oddly shaped gun from the special holster beneath his coat.

It was one of the machine pistols that all the aids of Doc Savage carried.

A gunman who appeared to be the leader of the mob—he was tall and solid-looking and grim—said, "I told you birds to be careful. These Doc Savage guys are dynamite. Now, watch it!"

Someone asked: "Doc Savage? Is *this* fellow one of Doc's men?"

"Boy!" added another. "We really got something, then!"

"What the hell you think we laid for this guy for?" demanded the big leader of the six thugs. "This'll kind of cool Doc Savage off when he hears about his college."

Ham stiffened. He was immediately prodded along, a gun stuck into his spine.

"What about Doc Savage's college?" the lawyer demanded as they reached the top of the bank.

Someone laughed. "He wants to know about the college!"

"Shuddup!"

Ham was given no information.

Instead, he and Honey Sanders were shoved along toward the woods which grew up close to the railroad cut. Someone used a flashlight, and the men were careful to see that the lawyer made no further fast moves.

After a while they came to a little shack located deep in the trees. It looked like an old structure used for the storing of tools. The single door of the structure was not even locked.

Inside the shack a lot of junk was piled around. The floor was of dirt.

Two of the gunmen started scuffing the dirt back with their feet, and shortly they were raising a trapdoor.

One man remarked, "Leaving this old dump unlocked like this has fooled others, too!"

Ham and the honey-haired girl were motioned toward the steps that led downward beneath the trap opening.

The passageway was damp and narrow. It finally ended in another flight of stairs leading upward. The big leader of the mob leaped ahead of Ham and the girl, went up the steps, grunted as he raised what must have been a heavy door. A length of iron chain jangled.

"All right; up!" he rapped from a room above.

The two captives were prodded up the steps and into a room about two dozen feet square. The walls of the place were solid-looking and of stone. There were no windows. There was no sign of a door.

The girl's frightened gaze flicked to Ham's. Understanding was mirrored in Honey Sander's deep-blue eyes. Ham knew what she was thinking.

This, obviously, was the impenetrable-looking stone house which they had looked over just a short while ago!

The leader stepped close to Ham and grinned. His jaw looked like something made carelessly out of cement.

"Brother," he said, "you got one out. You can pitch in with us and give us some information. Where's Doc Savage?"

Perhaps none saw the expression that came into the lean-waisted lawyer's eyes. For any mention of hobnobbing with crooks caused Ham to see red. He exploded into action.

His trained, fast-moving fists knocked two men to the ground before they knew what hit them. A third followed. The other three piled on Ham and drove him back against one stone wall of the veritable prison. A gun butt crashed against his cheek, struck again at his jaw. He fell down in a dazed heap.

Honey Sanders screamed.

"O. K., bud," the leader snapped. "You can stay here and *rot!* Sooner or later, Oscar's goin' to get Doc Savage anyway!"

The big fellow nodded to his companions and they started back down through the trap entranceway. He followed, and light went out of the room as the flashlight glow disappeared and the heavy trapdoor—it must have been made of steel—clanked down into place. Beneath it, a chain rattled as a padlock was fastened.

Ham got groggily to his feet. He heard the girl sobbing.

He realized suddenly that he had been mistaken in thinking this attractive girl was a phony. He said musingly, into the darkness that smashed all around them:

"I wonder who this guy Oscar is—the one they're going to put on Doc's trail?"

The girl was close to him, because Ham heard the startled intake of her breath.

"Oscar," she gasped, "is . . . is that flying *thing!*"

Chapter IV

LANTERNS IN THE NIGHT

Doc Savage had his first contact with "Oscar" at a point approximately six thousand feet over western New Jersey. But first, something else occurred before the bronze man got involved with the mysterious flying menace.

The bronze giant had been piloting the plane alone. Small mountains sprawled like bumps on a molehill far below him. There was no wind, and the night was good for flying.

Relaxed, his metallic features appearing like something made out of pure bronze, Doc had set the automatic robot pilot and the ship was flying itself. The course was set to follow a radio beam which would bring him into New York in about half an hour.

The short-wave loud-speaker—which the bronze giant had kept turned on, just in case there should be any routine call from any of his five aides—suddenly crackled.

Doc Savage turned a dial, asked quietly, "Yes?"

"Calling Doc Savage!" an excited man's voice said. *"Urgent message for Doc Savage!"*

The tone of the man's voice brought Doc up tensely in the cockpit seat.

"Doc Savage speaking," he said into a microphone. "Proceed."

"This is Dr. Nelson, Mr. Savage," the voice continued swiftly. *"I'm speaking from the college. Something's happened here that you ought to know!"*

If the bronze man was upset by the announcement, the fact was not expressed on his features. But there was one slight indication showing that his remarkable brain had sharpened—Doc's unusual eyes brightened imperceptibly.

Those eyes were striking because of their strange coloring. Like pools of rich flake-gold, they stirred continuously, as though affected by soft winds.

Likewise, the bronze giant's features and hair were of this unusual metallic hue, the hair being slightly darker than the skin of Doc's face. The hands that gripped the microphone were also bronze-colored; large, sinewy hands that revealed an inner strength far beyond the ordinary.

"You might explain," Doc told the medical man of his "college" in upstate New York. For Doctor Nelson was one of the staff of trained surgeons that the bronze man kept at his remarkable institution.

"There was an explosion," the man went on rapidly. *"We have not been able to learn what caused it. One corner of the main building has been demolished!"*

"Any casualties?" Doc said.

"Yes. One. An attendant who was down at the end of the hall. And two other attendants were hurt, Mr. Savage. Luckily, though, there were no patients in the corner rooms where the explosion occurred. But there—"

There was something in the last word that held Doc's attention. As it trailed off, the bronze man said quickly, "Yes? What else?"

"One of the patients has escaped," continued the doctor worriedly. *"A man named Birmingham Jones. Perhaps you recall his history—"*

"Yes," the bronze man put in. "Go on."

It was not necessary for Dr. Nelson to repeat pertinent facts about the patient named Birmingham Jones."

In his remarkable memory, Doc Savage carried a case history of every crook who had ever been sent to his "college." He recalled now that Birmingham Jones had been a gangster, outlaw, murderer—a former member of notorious gangs that had roamed the Middle West.

Only recently had Birmingham Jones been caught by Doc himself, and sent to the institution to undergo the bronze man's delicate brain treatments—operations that removed all memory of a criminal past, and that fitted crooks for worthwhile, honest careers in society.

But in the case of Birmingham Jones, Doc remembered that the dangerous crook had hardly had time to undergo the full course of treatments!

"He escaped?" Doc rapped.

"As clean as a whistle!" said the voice on the air. *"Our guards have scoured the woods and every inch of ground. We are now convinced that he was met by someone with a car. But there is no trace of them."*

"Anything else?" Doc prodded.

"No, sir. We have everything under control here now. But I wanted you to know about this man Birmingham Jones."

Doc listened a moment longer, then ended this conversation with the doctor. At the moment, he was not needed at his "college." Of more importance, was to learn the whereabout of one Birmingham Jones!

He quickly tuned in on his New York headquarters, where his five aides should be.

And static abruptly filled the short-wave set and made contact impossible. Doc's eyes narrowed, for the night was clear enough that reception should be perfect.

He checked the radio beam on which the plane was

flying. He was right on the beam into New York, but—

But something else was also interfering with that beam, destroying any chance of getting a radio call through!

Doc frowned slightly, and his gaze happened to flick ahead through the cockpit windows. He saw the object streaking down the sky directly in his path!

For a scant instant, slight puzzlement was mirrored in the bronze man's flake-gold eyes. For he knew that any commercial plane flying west—in the opposite direction to his own—should either be two thousand feet above or below him. That was aviation law.

And yet—

The other ship was hurtling right at his ship, unswerving, making no slightest attempt to avoid a smashup!

When it seemed that a collision was a certainty, Doc Savage put his own fast plane into a wing turnover, side slipped, then sent his craft plunging downward in a furious power dive.

The object that streaked overhead made a peculiar shrill whistling sound in the night.

And as it passed, Doc had straightened out of the fast dive and was zooming for altitude again. With the nose of his streamlined ship pointing upward, his intent gaze tried to make out the design of the thing that had almost crashed into him.

Far off in the night sky, he had a vague glimpse of the speeding object turning, of seeing it return on the course that the bronze man had been following.

It was traveling faster than the fastest plane made! Within seconds, it seemed, it had disappeared again into the east.

The bronze giant reached a hand toward the control panels as he leveled the ship off and headed eastward himself. He was adjusting a radio direction-finder.

In a moment, he picked up the sound of the rocket of a thing that had disappeared. Keeping the sound carefully tuned in, Doc followed the same course.

And he understood now why he had been unable to contact his New York headquarters. The thing that had almost struck his own plane had interfered with that contact, had created the static.

Also, if anyone human had been flying the rocketing object, he must be completely crazy. Thus the bronze man decided to investigate—if only to save other plane pilots from destruction!

The trail—Doc was still using the direction-finder and managing to keep the escaping thing somehow charted—ended over the Hudson River.

The exact vicinity was near a wide expanse of the river near Tarrytown. Old legends came to the bronze man's mind.

Legends of Sleepy Hollow and the headless horseman!

It was just over the peaceful-looking, slumbering communities strung along the river shore below, that Doc Savage lost all trail of the thing he had been following.

All sound in the direction-finder device had abruptly stopped. It meant only one thing.

The bronze man must have flown into the "dead" spot that would be directly over where the other flying machine had disappeared. And this meant—the river itself.

Doc Savage immediately cut his motors, started circling downward in long spirals. He carried no riding lights now. With the motors idling, the bronze man heard no other sound in the vast solitude of the night.

But as he dropped closer to the dark waters of the river, he saw the cluster of lights along the east bank. Not lights of houses—for the few that he observed were in darkness—but bobbing fireflies that would indicate moving lanterns.

Closer now, Doc saw that men were carrying the lanterns and apparently looking for something near the river's edge.

He set the amphibian plane smoothly down on the

water and taxied toward shore, at a point some distance above where the group of men were moving about mysteriously in the night.

Doc brought the amphibian as close to shore as was possible, and then dropped an anchor mooring into the shallow water.

But before leaving the plane, he took certain small gadgets from an equipment case stored in the cabin, placed these in a special vest that he wore beneath his suit coat.

The vest—it was one containing a number of pockets—was an equipment vest that the bronze man was seldom without.

He walked through knee-deep water, climbed over rocks that formed the roadbed of the railroad and started back to where he had last seen the men with the lanterns.

The bronze man did not seem to hurry, and yet he covered ground at amazing speed. He followed, silently, a cinder pathway that bordered the smooth rails.

His idea was to take by surprise those who had been acting so strangely near the river bank.

That must have been the general idea of the men with the lanterns. They piled on Doc Savage as he passed over a small trestle that spanned a tiny creek leading into the river.

Chapter V

TRAP

The group of husky-looking fellows, minus their lanterns, had been waiting, crouched down, beside a pathway that led down beneath the low trestle. Assorted hands grabbed hold of the bronze man.

Someone said, "This is the guy, like I told you! He came down in that plane!"

That seemed to be sufficient to start the battle. With grunts and curses, the group smashed into Doc.

One man took hold of the bronze man's right arm and attempted to twist it up in a hammer lock. He stopped abruptly, as though he might have run up against a stone wall. Amazement made small saucers of his popping eyes.

He found the bronze man's right arm a piece of immovable cement beneath his powerful grip. He landed flat on his back as a flick of that same arm threw him clear.

The same thing happened to a man who attempted to seize the bronze giant's left arm.

Two others leaped at Doc Savage's legs. A third climbed on his back.

Incredible, blurred movement followed. The newcomer threw the attackers off so fast that it was hard to tell just how he had accomplished it. But within seconds, five figures lay on the ground beside the railroad ties and gasped for breath.

The sixth man—he had remained clear—walked up to the big fellow, sprayed the glow of a flashlight over the bronze man's features, and exclaimed, "Oh, blow me down for a fool. There's been an awful mistake. *You're Doc Savage!*"

"It appears that there has been an error," said the bronze man quietly, and he stood unmoving as the other men picked themselves up lamely and grouped around the short, stockily built man who had just spoken.

The stocky man wore tweeds that were in outrageous contrast to his I am-going-to-a-fire necktie. He had short-clipped hair like bristly wheat straw, and there was an evil-smelling pipe stuck into his ruddy face.

"Yes," he repeated worriedly, "there's been an awful mistake. We thought you were one of them. You see"—he waved a hand to indicate those with him

—"these chaps are deputized lawmen. They are part of the posse."

"Posse?" The bronze giant's face was without changeable expression.

And as the various men picked themselves up and stared in awe at the metallic figure, their eyes widened. Because, standing apart from others, Doc Savage's physique did not seem unusual. This was because of the perfect symmetry of his muscular development.

The ruddy-faced man with the foul pipe was continuing excitedly. "Yes, posse," he said. He explained about the girl who had disappeared—Honey Sanders. He introduced himself.

"Me, I'm Sandy Gower. I'm constable in these here parts, Mr. Savage." The stocky, important lawman's chest seemed to stick out farther. "I left that fellow waiting while I went back to see about his damaged car. And now *he's* gone! I don't know what we'll do about that battling partner of his, that Monk or whatever they call him. He's—"

The bronze figure's eyes sharpened.

"You said Monk?" Doc demanded quickly.

"Yep. A bad egg."

Briefly, Sandy Gower explained about the smashup and how Monk had landed behind bars of the local jail. He added little further to enlighten Doc Savage as to why Monk and Ham Brooks had been up here in Sleepy Hollow, save to interview a girl named Honey Sanders.

Doc listened quietly, then he announced, "The one called Ham, who you say has disappeared, is one of my aides. As is the one you say is now in jail."

The red-faced constable's eyes bulged.

"Oh, my gosh!" he cried. And then, "Say, Doc Savage, I didn't know that fellow Monk was in your organization, or I wouldn't have—"

"Monk," Doc said quietly, "sometimes runs into difficulties. Perhaps we should see him."

Sandy Gower almost fell over himself trying to be accommodating. He led the way back to his dilapidated flivver, after assigning his deputized men to continue the search for either Honey Sanders or the Doc Savage aide named Ham Brooks.

Perhaps the constable knew—since he was a small-town law officer himself—that the bronze man held an honorary commission on the New York police force. In that city, Doc Savage had the authority of any police official.

At the jail, Doc Savage offered to pay Monk's bail. But Constable Sandy Gower would not hear of it.

He explained how Ham Brooke had already, through him, paid for any damages caused at the oil station; and that the garageman had stated he could have the car in running condition before dawn. Because he had been more than well paid for any damages, he had been willing to work the remainder of the night on the car.

Monk, a grin threatening to dislodge his ears, came out of the open cell and let out a whoop at sight of Doc.

"How did you know—" he started in his childlike, piping voice.

"That will take some explaining—later," Doc Savage said as he started to lead the way out.

"But where's Ham?" Monk wanted to know.

"We will try to find him."

Sandy Gower, the constable, interjected, "Hell's bells! I figured this Monk and the one called Ham for deadly enemies!"

"As a matter of fact," the bronze man said, "they are the best of friends."

But Monk was glaring at the rotund, stocky constable.

"Lookit, you overstuffed kewpie!" he said belligerently. "When I find that shyster Ham, I'm gonna twist off his ears!"

Sandy Gower stared after hairy Monk as, with a waddling, gorilla-like gait, he followed the bronze man out. The constable was flabbergasted at hearing that those two strange fellows, Monk and Ham, could possibly be friends.

But he might have changed his opinion could he have seen Monk half an hour later.

With Doc Savage, the hairy chemist was intent on scouring the vicinity not far from the white cottage of Honey Sanders, in Sleepy Hollow. So far, there had been no trace of the girl or the lawyer, Ham.

Monk, in the meantime, had informed the bronze man about their trip up here; of seeing the strange hobgoblin of a thing that had zoomed so close over their car.

As Monk explained, his little eyes popping in his incredibly homely face, "Blazes, Doc, the danged thing must 'a' been that headless horseman. Only he was ridin' some kind of a barrel—a long skinny barrel with wings—"

They had been proceeding along the river bank, not far from a small stone building that had no visible means of entrance. The bronze man was using a device that he had removed from one of his coat pockets.

Shaped like a very small, boxlike lantern, the device used an infrared ray principle in revealing footprints in the darkness.

The moon had slid down in the west, and it was the dark hour before dawn. Chill dampness floated in from the nearby Hudson River.

The bronze man was bent over as he walked carefully, examining the ground. Abruptly he paused, leaned closer to the earth and said quietly, "The girl was with him."

"With who?" Monk asked.

"Ham." Doc was making measurements with his fingers. "They are Ham's shoes. The width and the length are exactly the same."

"The blasted shyster!" Monk piped. "That's why he left me there in jail—so he could meet that girl alone!"

The pair of footprints—fresh in the dew-wet grass of night—did not lead past the blockhouse-type, small stone building. They seemed to come from the woods beyond, skirted the small structure and continued down the embankment at some distance away from what was a frequently used dirt path.

Doc Savage followed, using the infrared device. At the crushed-stone roadbed of the railroad, the prints disappeared, but the bronze man picked them up again across the tracks. They led right down to the water's edge.

There was a bit of sandy beach close to the rock fill beneath the railroad bed. A mark in the damp sand showed that a rowboat had recently been tied up here. There was another rowboat nearby, turned upside down with its bow resting on a boulder.

Doc Savage looked at the flat, exposed bottom of the rowboat and a strange sound came from his lips.

It could be best described as a trilling, soft and musical; low, mellow, it was like the rare song of some bird of the jungle.

The sound was one that Doc had made in moments of startling discovery or danger.

Monk tensed. "What is it, Doc?"

"A message from Ham," said Doc Savage. "It was left for you."

The bronze giant was studying what was apparently invisible writing made with some sort of special crayon. The device which he held in his hand apparently made the words visible.

"Ham," Doc went on, "has rowed out to what he states is a boat moored across the river. He says the mystery of the flying thing has something to do with that boat. You were to follow if you found his message."

Monk was standing, staring out over the water. His small eyes appeared to be closed in his scarred features as he squinted into the gloom.

"Don't see no boat," announced Monk.

Doc Savage, too, was looking. He remained motionless for several moments, his attention on the river.

Finally he said, "It's not exactly a boat, but rather a barge, lying low in the water. It's very close to the far shore. We had better investigate."

But first, the bronze man led the way upriver to where his amphibian plane was moored. It was not more than half a mile away.

They waded out to the ship, climbed aboard.

Doc directed, "Cast off. We will taxi quietly upstream and across to a point above the barge. Then we can approach the barge by drifting silently down with the outgoing tide."

The dampness of the small strip of sandy beach back by the rowboat had informed Doc that the tide was still running out.

Ten minutes later, they were close to the opposite banks of the Hudson. Doc Savage killed the softly humming engines. Like a phantom of the night, the plane drifted downstream under cover of darkness.

Shortly, Monk saw the outlines of the barge directly ahead. Carrying no lights, it lay well out of the regular river channels, close to steep, wooded banks that rose up from the shore.

Getting up from the cockpit seat, Doc motioned Monk into his place.

He ordered, "Wait ten minutes, or until you see a flashlight signal, then taxi the plane up to the barge. In the meantime, keep quiet."

"What're you gonna do?" Monk wanted to know.

But in the next moment, Doc's appearance supplied the answer to Monk's worried question.

For the bronze man had put on a helmet-type thing that looked like an inverted, large fish bowl. The device was fitted with a small oxygen tank that strapped across the shoulders, and with a mouth-breathing tube.

The plane was perhaps four hundred yards from the barge when Doc Savage stepped overside and disappeared beneath the surface of the river.

Monk waited anxiously. He knew that the bronze giant was swimming below the surface, in a cautious approach to the mysterious, unlighted barge.

What would he find there? Ham? The girl?

Restless, Monk waited. Five minutes. Ten.

To himself, he murmured, "Doggone it, Doc should 'a' been there five minutes ago!"

Abruptly, Monk stiffened at the sound of the high, shrill whine that came out of the night. His mouth fell open. His little eyes popped. For he recognized the familiar shriek of the hobgoblin flying thing!

Then the flash of light came.

But it was not the beam of a flashlight that Monk had been waiting for.

Instead, a sheet of red brilliance spurted upward for a hundred feet into the sky. It made red lava color of the river surface and illuminated the shore for half a mile either way.

It was followed by the terrific detonation that almost flung Monk out of the plane cockpit seat. He saw the planking and debris that was thrown up into the air.

The barge, blown into thousands of flying pieces, was no more.

Chapter VI

MESSAGE FROM HAM

A few seconds later, wreckage started raining down on the plane in which Monk was seated. Since the outer skin of the ship was of a new-type metal alloy, no damage was done.

The only trouble was that the dropping planks and parts of the exploded barge kept Monk from getting immediately out of the cabin.

Monk stalked up and down the small space, his hairy hands balled in tight knots, his eyes filled with something that was almost grief.

"Blazes!" he moaned. "They must 'a' tricked Doc!"

Timber kept thumping down on the cabin's metal

roof. But after a while it stopped, and the chemist leaped to the door. As he swung it open, he heard the whine of the flying hobgoblin of a thing. He jerked back with a start.

And then Monk saw that he had been mistaken. What had made the roar was an inboard speedboat with a streamlined hull. The boat was just swinging up beside the amphibian plane bobbing gently around on the water.

Three men were in the cockpit of the speed craft, and obviously—figuring that Doc Savage must have arrived alone in his plane, and was now dead—they had come out to take over.

With a howl of rage, Monk leaped clear of the plane and landed in the bottom of the speedboat. The three men were not carrying guns in their hands; they had not expected to meet anyone aboard the drifting plane.

Burly fingers fell on the stocky chemist. Someone kicked Monk in the face.

Monk let out a bull-like roar and grabbed two heads. He started shaking the two fellows as though they might have been sawdust-filled rag dolls.

Soon, completely dazed, they staggered around in the cockpit of the boat. Monk cocked a fist, slammed it into the third man's face and watched him flop back into a leather-cushioned seat.

The other two had lost enough of their dizziness to leap in at Monk once again.

Monk tapped one of the men on the chin. The man fell on his back, sprawled across the one who was already unconscious on the leather seat. The chemist's powerful hands quickly scooped down and dragged the fellow up by the collar.

But the man's eyes were still closed. There was no fight left in him.

Monk swore. Unable to restrain his impulsiveness, he hit the big guy again just for good luck. Monk was like that. He always believed in doing a good job.

He was aware that the third man had been trying to climb on his neck, from somewhere behind him. Monk whirled, letting go with a terrific haymaker.

But he missed.

He missed because the third man had leaped clear, was swinging a long boat hook at the same instant the chemist let drive the roundhouse swing.

Monk lost his balance, the heavy boat hook caught him behind the ear, and he tumbled overboard into the river.

The man in the boat dropped his weapon, leaped to the wheel of the craft and gunned the motor. He looked back, grinning as he saw the spot where the black river had closed over Monk's disappearing head.

"That's that!" he snarled, and the craft beneath him streaked downstream.

It took more than a bop on the head to knock out the scrappy chemist, however.

His brain cleared the moment he struck the cool water. Monk remembered to hold his breath as he went below the surface. From the drumming sound that was in his eardrums, he realized that the speedboat had already made an escape.

And so he held his breath as long as he could, hanging just beneath the surface. Monk had an idea—since the crooks had escaped anyway—that it might be a good thing to let them think he was drowned. No telling when he would meet up with them again—and Monk was already planning a little surprise reception.

He broke surface sputtering, his bright, small eyes peering around him. The speedboat was nowhere visible, but from a distance came the powerful, slowly fading purr of the speed craft.

Monk struck out for the plane and a few moments later was climbing aboard. He was thinking of Doc Savage, of the fact that the bronze man must have been blown to bits in the barge explosion. Monk's shoulders sagged hopelessly as he swung open the door to the cabin of the ship.

Doc Savage said quietly, "I could have fired some shots at that speedboat, but there was too much danger of hitting you."

Monk stared, then he let out a whoop of joy.

"Doc! Goshamighty, I thought you was blasted to hell an' gone when that barge let go!"

Doc Savage had just taken off the glass-bowl diving helmet and was storing it away in a case, along with the breathing apparatus that went with the device.

He straightened, and said, "It was obvious that the barge might be some sort of trap."

And then the bronze man explained that he had not proceeded directly to the barge. Instead, he had swum underwater and reached the rocky shore at a point some distance north of the darkened boat. There, he had waited, hidden in darkness, suspecting that he might have been seen as he dropped overside from his plane.

Monk gulped. "Goshamighty!" he piped. "Somebody expected you to appear on the barge, an' they had that reception waiting for you!"

Doc nodded. "It appears so."

The bronze man, his clothing still soaking wet, stepped toward the cockpit. "It might be best to return to headquarters," he said. "There is no trace of Ham or the girl here. But Ham might have escaped and returned to New York. Later, someone can drive your car down from that gas station."

Monk, seated beside the bronze man as the plane took off, looked worried. His eyes were solemn.

"You think," he prodded, "Ham might have been on that barge, Doc?"

Doc Savage was silent a moment, busy with the controls.

Then he said quietly, "It is doubtful. If Ham is a captive, he is probably being held somewhere else. The barge was not blown up by anyone near it."

"But how—" the chemist started.

He paused, seeing that Doc was thinking of something else. Also, it was a habit of the bronze giant not to make explanations until he had the complete solution to a problem.

He said now, "We might be able to locate the men in the speedboat. They are obviously connected with the mystery."

Thoughts of catching up with the three crooks again brought a new gleam to Monk's little eyes.

"Yeah," he rapped. "Let's find 'em."

But they found no trace of the fast speedboat, though Doc Savage even flew close to the water and covered both shore lines of the Hudson.

And as they neared New York, the towns along the shore grew more numerous. There were dozens of boat landings where the fast craft might have put in. Also, they flew over at least half a dozen yacht clubs, where scores of small boats were tied up in the water near shore. The speedboat could easily have been concealed among others of like design.

Doc continued toward Manhattan.

Dawn was making striking silhouettes of New York's skyline when the bronze man finally set the amphibian down and taxied toward his water-front hangar.

The skyscraper headquarters of Doc Savage was located on the eighty-sixth floor of a downtown office building. A private, high-speed elevator whisked Doc and Monk swiftly to the topmost floor of the building.

The headquarters consisted of three rooms. Few persons had even been farther than the first—the reception room. This was fairly small, and contained a large safe, comfortable chairs and a huge inlaid table. The other two rooms were much larger.

One was a library, its walls lined with scientific volumes covering anything that had ever been accomplished in science and medicine.

The third immense room was Doc Savage's private laboratory. It was the envy of the few great scientists who had ever been privileged to see it.

The unhealthy-looking fellow who arose, stifling a yawn, from a deep chair in the reception room, appeared like a prospect for an embalming school.

His skin was sallow, his long bony body looked as though a stiff wind would put kinks in it. He had thin blond hair and pale-blue eyes. His forehead, however, was tremendous.

He said, "Golly, Doc, there's been the devil to pay! I've been waiting for you!"

Monk had flopped into a chair. He squinted at the skinny man and asked, "Hey, Long Tom, you heard anything from Ham?"

The skinny one turned his attention to the hairy chemist and gave a snort of disgust. "When you two left here last night, I figured you would probably run into trouble. What's happened now?"

Monk gave a sour grimace. "That shyster Ham," he said, "has gone and got himself involved with a girl—"

Doc Savage interrupted quietly, "You were going to tell us something, Long Tom?"

The skinny man's eyes looked worried as he turned his attention from Monk.

"Yes," he said swiftly. "It's about something that happened at the college upstate." And he related what Doc Savage had already heard in the radio message to his plane.

Long Tom was another of the bronze man's aides. His full title was Major Thomas J. Roberts. He was the electrical wizard in the bronze giant's remarkable group of worldwide adventurers.

And strangely, for all his unhealthy appearance, he was a wiry bundle of piano-wire muscles and speed. When aroused, he could fight like a demon. He had never known a sick day in all his life.

Monk was suddenly out of the chair, listening to Long Tom's story of the mysterious explosion at Doc's college. He heard about the escape of a former criminal named Birmingham Jones.

Long Tom added: "I've been in contact with the college all night. Birmingham Jones has not been found."

Doc told, briefly, of what had happened up the Hudson near Sleepy Hollow. He mentioned the barge explosion.

It was Monk, suddenly excited, who put in, "Say, that's funny! Two explosions—a couple hundred miles apart! Maybe—"

But Long Tom was busy adding another detail of the college explosion for Doc's benefit.

"There was something else," the electrical wizard was saying. "A peculiar, shrill whistling sound just before the explosion happened. They have not discovered what it was, Doc."

The bronze man's eyes were thoughtful. "Whistling sound?"

"Yes. It—"

Monk let out a yell. "Doc! That's the noise that blasted goblin of a flyin' thing made over Sleepy Hollow. An' I betcha it was the same thing I heard just before that danged barge went sky-high!"

Doc Savage nodded without speaking. He said nothing about the mysterious object that had almost crashed into his plane as he had been flying toward New York.

Instead, he queried, "This girl Honey Sanders that you mentioned, Monk? There was something about her seeing some sort of flying apparition near Sleepy Hollow, of her being hysterical and badly frightened?"

Monk jerked his head. He started to reach in his pocket, then swore. "Blast it!" he rapped. "Ham's got her picture. It was in the papers last night!"

Doc suggested, "It might be a good idea to buy another paper, Monk."

The chemist started for the door, to go down to the street. He returned five minutes later with a morning edition. He was excited. Not because he had found anything about Honey Sanders—the story, apparently, had been dropped—but because of the headlines that were on the first page.

Monk pointed at the heavy black type, and said tensely, "Blazes, Doc! Lookit this!"

The item read:

MYSTERY
SURROUNDS PLANT
EXPLOSION IN NEW JERSEY

Early this morning, a mysterious blast rocked a part of the vast cellulose plant located at Mayville, in the New Jersey meadows a few miles out of New York City.

Police say that it was only through an act of Providence that the teriffic explosion took place a scant hour before five hundred men would have been at work in the building which was demolished.

Sabotage has been hinted, but officials of the industrial concern deny all such possibilities. But it has been noted that the cellulose concern manufactures a product used in war, and now residents are recalling the Black Tom explosions that occurred in the vicinity during the last World War.

Cornelia Duval, millionaire industrialist and director of the firm, could not be located at an early hour this morning. It was thought that he might have a statement to make.

And further on, near the bottom of the long news account, was a brief paragraph which said:

Jules Smith, watchman at the plant, who was fortunate to be making his rounds at some distance from where the actual explosion took place, and who was not hurt, told of a peculiar shrill whistling sound that he heard just before the blast. He was unable to say exactly what the sound was, though he was positive that it came from the sky.

Monk, who had been reading over Long Tom's shoulder, let out a squeal.

"Golly!" he exploded. "Maybe this has got something to do with that explosion up the river, Doc! Maybe—"

"Or," the bronze man put in, "it might be pure coincidence. That watchman was more than likely excited by the explosion, and he might have imagined things."

"But—" the chemist started, and the ringing of the phone interrupted him.

Doc Savage picked up the receiver. A second later, he said swiftly, "Yes, Ham?"

Monk, listening, jumped up and down happily. "Then that shyster's O. K.?" he asked.

Doc, listening at the phone, nodded. He listened attentively, finally said, "It should take us about thirty minutes to get there," and then hung up.

"Get where, Doc?" Monk asked anxiously.

"It seems," stated Doc Savage, "that Ham and the girl—Honey Sanders—are safe." There was a certain brightness to the bronze giant's flake-gold, magnetic eyes. "Ham has a lead to the flying thing. He is waiting for us now."

As Doc Savage started toward the door, it was Long Tom who asked, "Waiting where?"

"At a spot just a half mile from where the explosion has occurred at the Duval plant in New Jersey!"

Chapter VII

GUY WITH A GUN

The quarter-mile-long manufacturing plant of Cornelius Duval, millionaire industrialist, was located in what had once been Jersey swamps along the old highway route to Newark. In recent years the lowlands had been filled in and numerous factories had been built in the area.

Cornelius Duval and his associates probably owned at least half of the industries located in the district.

The building of this particular unit, which had been half demolished, was a processing shop located far down near one corner of the string of shops. Motorcycle police patrolled the roadway just outside the high wire fence now, and no one had been permitted entrance except a few plant officials.

The place where Ham Brooks had asked Doc Savage to meet him was at a road-stand place at some dis-

tance from the damaged shop. The construction of a
new highway had long since put the small eating place
out of business. It was deserted.

Ham and the girl were seated on the rear steps of
the old wooden building when Doc Savage and the others arrived in the bronze man's limousine. Outwardly,
the somber appearance of the machine would hardly
indicate that it was armor-proof, or that the windows
would resist machine-gun bullets.

Doc and skinny Long Tom were introduced to the
girl by Ham, who told briefly of what had happened
since he had met pretty Honey Sanders.

It appeared that after they had been seized by the
six gunmen in Sleepy Hollow, and left locked in the
stone-walled prison, a man had been sent back to question the girl about her interview with newspaper reporters.

Ham had managed to knock the fellow out, and he
and Honey Sanders had escaped, to later follow the other gunmen in the night and overhear a conversation
that involved Doc Savage.

As Ham now started to exclaim, "It was about your
college upstate, Doc. There was an explosion, and
somehow those birds knew about it. They said—"

The bronze man nodded. "Yes. We have already
learned about the trouble up there," he said
quietly.

Ham went on worriedly. "But that isn't all. A guy
named Birmingham Jones escaped from the college. It
seems he was to grab Honey Sanders"—Ham smiled
at the girl—"but then these guys decided this Birmingham Jones was to have a different assignment, seeing as
they already had the girl."

"Different?" asked Doc Savage. "What do you
mean?"

"Birmingham Jones was to be sent over here to Jersey, to this very plant where the explosion happened
early this morning!" announced the lawyer. "We managed to follow them toward a spot where they were
to meet this Birmingham Jones, but later we lost the
trail. So we came over here, seeing as Honey Sanders,

here, knows something about a man named Patrick Valentine."

Monk was suddenly excited. "Golly, Doc!" he piped in his shrill voice. "I'll bet that Birmingham Jones was the one blew up this place!"

But the bronze man shook his head.

"Hardly that," he said, but he did not explain this remark. Instead, he looked at the slender, pretty girl.

"You said something about a man named Patrick Valentine?"

The girl shook her head swiftly, her blue eyes wide.

"Yes. That's what they call him, but I have an idea the name is a fake."

"Fake?"

"I mean, one used to shield his real identity. He must be a devil!"

The bronze man's eyebrows raised slightly. "Why do you say that?"

"Because Patrick Valentine—whoever he is—is behind all this trouble. I've overheard enough to know this is true. Patrick Valentine is planning something that is going to shock half the world. What, I don't know. But it *is* something big!"

For a moment, Doc Savage was thoughtful. Then he indicated the limousine, which he had parked well behind the road stand while Monk had first been arguing with Ham.

"Monk can stay here with the girl," Doc directed. "It might be a good idea for the rest of us to try to learn just what Birmingham Jones was doing at the Duval plant."

The bronze man looked at the unhealthy-appearing electrical wizard. "Long Tom, you and Ham might try to get into that shop where the explosion occurred. Find out what took place."

Long Tom asked, "Doc, about that phone call you stopped off to make on the way over here? Has it anything to do with—"

"The call was to Cornelius Duval," explained the bronze man. "He has an appointment with me at the plant in ten minutes."

Doc consulted his watch. "Meet back here at the car in an hour."

Doc Savage then disappeared toward the plant of the millionaire manufacturer. Ham and Long Tom followed.

Someone had once said that Ham Brooks should have been an orator. He could talk. And his legal training made his arguments convincing, when he wished them to be.

His words convinced the watchman stationed at one of the Duval plant gates.

"No one gets inside the grounds!" the watchman had insisted. "Them's orders!"

But now the man was saying, "Well, if you two are insurance-company examiners, like you say, I guess I'll have to let you. But you be careful. Part of that building hasn't collapsed yet—but it's liable to!"

Ham and Long Tom entered the grounds inside the high wire fence.

The building they shortly approached lay, mostly a pile of bricks, on the ground. At least, half of it did.

The remainder—a structure several stories high— showed one slightly bulging wall.

In a large storage yard off to the left, outside the part of the shop that had collapsed, was the remains of what had been a huge vat of some type. There was an odor of chemicals in the air.

Long Tom said, "That tank must have been knocked right through the walls of the building. Funny! The products they manufacture here are not explosive."

They moved on, located a small exit door in the wall of the part of the shop still standing. Long Tom led the way inside.

They saw machines and equipment that had been smashed to pieces. The smell of spilled chemicals in here was stronger, causing the two men to cough occasionally.

Ham remarked, "Lucky these employees had not yet come to work. Otherwise, hundreds of them would have been killed."

Long Tom nodded, saying nothing. He had been sniffing the air as they walked through the shop, past various vats and beneath massive overhead pipes that were obviously used as liquid conveyers.

"Can't quite place it," Long Tom remarked, his thin, sensitive nose screwed up as he still sniffed.

"Place what?" Ham asked.

"The odor. Like burned ozone. It's something that was hardly caused by the chemicals which they use here."

Ham said, "If only some of those employees were here, perhaps they could give us an idea what it might be."

From above the slender lawyer's head, the grating voice rapped, "Brother, maybe *we* can help you!"

Ham jerked back, staring upward at the big pipe lines that ran overhead through the shop.

Assorted forms came tumbling down on him and Long Tom.

The assailants wore dungarees and workmen's caps. But their faces were the kind that are found in rogues' galleries.

Long Tom and Ham were seized and carried by sheer weight of falling bodies to the floor of the shop. One of the attackers remarked confidently, "Who said these Doc Savage mugs are tough? Why, hell, they're just set-ups—"

The one speaking was on top of bony Long Tom. He never finished the sentence; perhaps never exactly knew what happened in the next split second.

He was thrown a dozen feet clear of the skinny electrical wizard's figure. Long Tom himself came off the floor like a piece of released spring steel. His pale eyes were glittering.

He grabbed another thug and began flattening the man's ears.

He knocked the second assailant flat. A third leaped on him.

Ham was holding his own with three more who had also come down off the overhead pipes. The well-dressed lawyer used no rough-house tactics. His fists merely appeared to flick out lightly.

But each blow was well aimed, deadly in its rapier-like suddenness.

Men fell down. Ham was soon dusting off his clothes and turning his attention to Long Tom, who had not done so badly himself. The electrical expert was just straightening from pounding the last thug senseless against the hard floor.

Ham started to comment, "Monk is going to feel hurt when he learns about this. Too bad he—"

The two men standing behind Long Tom and Ham laughed. They both held guns.

One said, "We kinda thought planting that phony watchman at the gate was a good idea."

He pulled the trigger of the gun in his hand.

Lead did not spurt from the weapon, but the liquid did, and it got into Ham's and Long Tom's eyes and they groped around blindly. The stuff had them momentarily helpless.

And while they were thus staggering about, the man with the liquid ammonia gun stepped forward, let a blackjack slide from his coat sleeve and started swinging.

The two Doc Savage aides were soon lying motionless on the floor.

The blackjack wielder said, "Soon as we can get enough of our punks awake to take care of these two, we'll go after Doc Savage."

Chapter VIII

ONE MAN WANTED

In the reception room outside the private office and conference chambers of Cornelius Duval, the cute little drugstore blonde sat at her switchboard and stared hopefully toward the bronze man seated across the small room. For ten minutes, the girl had been giving hopeful sighs as she gazed at Doc Savage.

Upon entering, Doc Savage had been informed by the girl that Cornelius Duval would see him in a few minutes. It appeared that a board meeting had been hurriedly ordered. Doc would be admitted to the conference room.

The blond receptionist was attractive enough to have to continually ward off passes made at her by every man who visited the general offices of Duval Industries.

But this giant bronze fellow had been one exception. He had hardly glanced at her. The girl was slightly deflated.

Three times, in the past five minutes, she had made remarks intended to draw the stranger into conversation.

But Doc had merely nodded, continuing to apparently stare at the walls. The receptionist could hardly know that the bronze fellow's expressionless features concealed the fact that his remarkable brain was intent on a problem.

For Doc was connecting various incidents that had happened throughout the night. He was thinking of a former crook and murderer named Birmingham Jones.

Birmingham Jones, obviously, was tied in with a mystery that was yet subtly hidden. Birmingham Jones, according to Ham's observations, had last headed toward the Duval plant.

That fact was puzzling. For Cornelius Duval, millionaire industrialist, was not the type of person to hobnob with crooks. One of the wealthiest men in America, Duval had developed many scientific products that had been useful to mankind. His record was one which leading citizens envied.

A buzzer sounded on the blond girl's switchboard. She plugged in one of the switchboard cords, murmured sweetly, "Ye-es?"

She listened a moment, then said, "He was here about half an hour ago. He has already seen Mr. Duval and has departed. . . . You're welcome."

The girl broke the connection.

Doc Savage was abruptly on his feet. The movement was casual, but the girl gave a start when she saw the giant bronze man standing near her desk. She had not heard Doc Savage move.

"Someone else has already seen Mr. Duval?" Doc queried.

The girl nodded. She was not supposed to give out such information. She merely smiled sweetly.

Doc Savage said, "Who was it? Can you recall the name?"

Something about the bronze figure's compelling eyes made the girl forget everything about rules and regulations. At that instant, she would even have gladly revealed her correct age.

She consulted a note pad on the switchboard. "It was a Mr. Birmingham Jones," she said sweetly.

If the information startled Doc Savage, his face showed no indication of the fact.

He merely said quietly, "Thank you," and started to move away from the receptionist's desk.

Her buzzer, at that moment, sounded again; and then she was saying, "You may go in now."

A middle-aged, businesslike woman met Doc Savage in the open doorway of a huge, expensively furnished office, nodded, led him through the room and into a chamber beyond.

A dozen men were seated around a long conference table. It was obvious that they had been talking excitedly in the moment just before the bronze man's entrance. Their faces were flushed; they looked warm.

The big man at the head of the table arose quickly, came forward and said pleasantly, "It's a pleasure to have this honor, Doc Savage." He shook hands.

Cornelius Duval had the aggressive manner of a man who has accomplished big things. He had steel-gray hair, a healthy outdoors look, and a handshake that befitted his rugged appearance.

Doc came swiftly to the point, outlining briefly the incident that happened at his "college" in upstate New

York. He referred casually to the crook named Birmingham Jones, spoke of the mysterious explosion that had taken place here at Duval's plant early this morning.

"Obviously," finished Doc Savage, "there is a connection between these unusual happenings—a connection involving one Birmingham Jones. Perhaps you are willing now to reveal information you hesitated to give out to the newspapers?"

Cornelius Duval, for a long moment, looked at the bronze man.

Then the heavy-set millionaire walked back to his place at the head of the board table. He remained standing, and his alert gray eyes flicked briefly over the group of men seated at the table. No one spoke.

Duval looked back at Doc Savage and said with emphasis, "The explosion at one of our shops this morning was an accident, Doc Savage. It was a thing that could happen in any industrial concern. It is nothing of great importance."

Something flickered in the bronze giant's eyes.

"And Birmingham Jones?" Doc Savage added quietly.

"I've never heard of the man," said Cornelius Duval, and there was something almost defiant in the millionaire's voice.

Doc's flake-gold eyes stirred restlessly. He nodded briefly, said, "Thank you," and moved toward the door.

Behind him, there was strained silence as he went out by way of Duval's private office.

Duval was obviously lying. Why? The blond receptionist had informed Doc Savage that a man named Birmingham Jones had seen the millionaire shortly before Doc himself. In that case—

On the way out through the outer office, Doc glanced toward the blond girl's desk. She was gone.

Doc rode an elevator down to the main-floor lobby of the building. There was a policeman standing just outside the elevator cab when the doors slid open.

He stared quickly at the bronze man, asked, "You're Doc Savage, aren't you?"

The cop was big, with a red face and thick-soled, large shoes.

Doc Savage nodded, glancing around the lobby of the building. At the moment, it was deserted.

"What is it?" Doc asked.

For Doc Savage at all times tried to avoid undue publicity. Naturally, in his dangerous career of righting wrongs and punishing evildoers, he was bound to draw public attention and acclaim. And yet he generally managed to remain in the background when newspaper publicity covered himself.

The policeman was quickly leading the way to where a prowl car was parked at the curb. His partner, a tall thin fellow in uniform, was waiting at the wheel of the car. The engine was running.

"Some of your men are in trouble!" informed the officer who had been waiting in the lobby. "It seems they tangled with some fake workmen who were planted in that exploded building of Duval's."

Doc listened, his eyes thoughtful.

"And we trailed the gang to a hide-out about a mile from here," went on the policeman. "One of your men got away from them, and told us to get you. I think his name was Monk."

The bronze man nodded, swung into the police car between the two officers. The tall driver immediately started up, wheeled the car around in the street and sent it streaking out of the small business-section which surrounded the factory main office.

Outside the town, they followed a rough road that had been the main highway in years past. But now the pavement was full of holes.

Houses dropped behind them; they came to a dismal section of low-lying marsh land and dumps. What had once been a huge gas-storage tank was located off to the right of the old road, set back in what was now a dumping grounds.

The driver swung the car in there, maneuvered the machine over a rutted roadway.

The gas-storage tank had long since been emptied of gas. Only one of its great circular sections rose up from the ground. The remainder of the tank had probably been dismantled.

The police car was parked nearby and the two officers jumped out, leading the way.

One said, "These birds must have fixed this tank up for a regular hide-out. Clever, eh?"

Doc agreed that it was.

They moved toward a heavy steel doorway built near the base of the old, rusted, drum-shaped tank. Nearing it, one of the policemen, said, "Listen!"

From inside the great tank, muffled but still audible, came sounds of what must be a terrific battle. One voice rose somewhat above the others—Monk's voice.

One of the cops said tensely, "That sounds like the fellow who called himself Monk!"

Doc nodded, standing aside as the heavier-set cop reached for a dog-arm latch that held the heavy door closed from the outside.

"We locked 'em in until we could get your help," said the officer, swinging open the door. "Come on—and be ready for a fight!"

As Doc hurried with the two men inside the tank, his right hand flicked to his vest, concealed beneath his coat.

When the door slammed behind them, and blinding light struck the bronze man's eyes, he flung out his arm as though to ward off the brilliant glow.

At the same time, the bronze giant gave a peculiar yell. The words were not understandable.

From beyond the blinding light, and magnified a hundred times by the vast emptiness inside the huge steel chamber, came an assortment of yells. The voices of Monk, Ham and skinny Long Tom!

But the aides stopped yelling abruptly. Strangely, they remained quiet.

But others in the circular, huge room did not. They kept fighting.

For they had not known that Doc Savage had spoken in an ancient Mayan tongue, which only he and his aides knew. What Doc had called was, "Hold your breaths!"

At the same moment, he seized the heavy-set cop next to him. With deceiving, smooth speed, the bronze giant hurled the big fellow to the ground, knocking him breathless.

Doc strained, to make a grab for the policeman's tall, slender partner.

But in the second that Doc Savage had made that peculiar outcry, and when his hands had flicked something into the air, the other cop had leaped back to the heavy entrance door.

It slammed even as Doc Savage turned, and the dog-arm handle twisted into place—from outside the tank.

Doc Savage stood still, apparently holding his breath, as he had been doing for a full moment.

After a moment, he relaxed and called out, "Careful! We can't be certain just how effective these anaesthetic gas bombs are in such a large space!"

From somewhere on the far side of the tank, from the darkness beyond the blinding light, came an explosive sigh as a man let out his breath. Monk's voice followed.

"Yeo-o-ow!" the hairy chemist squalled. "Look at 'em!"

Doc had moved swiftly toward the blinding light, learned that it was a 300-watt bulb placed in a movable stand. He now swung the light around to shine across the big enclosed space of the old tank.

Monk, grinning, was sitting astride a heap of limp figures. Some of those who were unconscious wore dungarees. They were the ones from the partially demolished factory building.

Ham and anaemic-looking Long Tom were standing guard over figures lying on the floor. Captives a moment ago, they were now in control.

The girl, attractive Honey Sanders, was lying down

with her head resting on an outflung arm, as though peacefully asleep.

For what the bronze man had used upon entering the hide-out was a form of small gas bomb of his own invention. The vials had been broken when Doc hurled them against the earth. The gas otherwise harmless, had the power to put people to sleep in the first moment that it mixed with the air.

Thus Doc had shouted the warning in Mayan, telling his aides to hold their breaths. Usually, the gas contained only knockout properties during the first moment or so.

The crooks sprawled out on the floor were already showing signs of returning consciousness.

Doc said, "Use their belts to tie them up."

Doc helped with the tying. He said, "We will question them later. But I doubt if they know much. They were probably just hired for this job by the man we want, and he has escaped."

Ham stared, "Escaped?"

Before Doc Savage could reply, Honey Sanders let out a long sigh and sat up.

She saw Doc Savage, and the expression of fear that had started to leap into her eyes disappeared.

Ham, always gallant, stepped forward swiftly to help the girl to her feet. Monk glared.

Honey Sanders said, "We thought they were policemen, and they grabbed Monk and then me. The real policemen, I heard them say, are tied up back there in the woods where your car is parked, Doc Savage!"

The bronze man nodded.

It was Long Tom who asked curiously, "But, Doc, how come those phony cops didn't fool you like they did Monk and the girl?"

"Because," offered the bronze giant, "one of the two was the man we want. There was something familiar about his face right from the first. He is the one who managed to leap back outside this place and escape." He moved toward the heavy door that had bolted from the outside. "It might be some time before we get out of here," the bronze man added.

"But who was it?" asked Ham, puzzled.

Doc announced: "That slender one who drove the stolen police car was Birmingham Jones!"

Chapter IX

"I KNOW VALENTINE!"

Getting information out of hard-boiled thugs was often one of the bronze man's problems. He had various scientific ways of doing this, when necessary. But a more simplified method—the one that usually got quick results—was Monk.

Monk didn't use much science. He employed his fists and a lot of fancy cuss words.

While Doc, Long Tom and Ham moved across the large tank room to see what they could do about opening the locked door, Monk was assigned to work over a few of the captives to see what information could be obtained from them.

Doc suggested that it might be a good idea if the girl, Honey Sanders, stepped across the room with them also. Shortly, hearing the racket behind her, she was glad she did so.

Fifteen minutes later—Long Tom and Ham were still working at the heavy steel door—Monk called out to Doc Savage. The bronze giant stepped back across the huge circular space.

Monk was standing with his hands on his hips, looking disgusted.

The captives were lined up along the inside of the tank wall, looking as though nothing else could ever possibly happen to them.

Monk growled, "What the heck! They're just a bunch of dumb roughnecks. Birmingham Jones hired them at twenty bucks a day to do some of his dirty work. They don't even know what this mystery is all about!"

Doc questioned some of the captives. The bronze man seemed more interested in learning about the mythical person who had been referred to by the girl as Patrick Valentine. Each of the battered-looking thugs was willing to talk.

"He's the big boss," said one.

"Birmingham works for that guy," put in another.

"Who is he?" demanded Doc.

They all shrugged. One remarked, "Damned if we know. But that's what they call him—Patrick Valentine."

Doc was thoughtful for a moment.

Monk stalked up and down before the bedraggled-looking line-up. His big fists were clenched at his sides.

"You birds gonna tell all you know, or do I go to work on you again?" he asked.

Each man cringed. Each had had sufficient samples of the hairy chemist's ability at getting information.

"That's *all* we know!" one captive offered. "Birmingham Jones was hired by this Patrick Valentine to handle some big deal. For all we know, Valentine could be anybody!"

Doc nodded to Monk. "They appear to be stating the truth," he said. "Tie them up again."

Long Tom and Ham had been unable to force the heavy steel door, the only escape from the tank room.

Honey Sanders' blue eyes were wide enough to show that she was scared. "What shall we *do?*" she asked, staring at Doc.

The bronze man ordered, "Everyone stand back."

Doc took something from the pocket of the special vest that he wore beneath his clothing. Next, he appeared to be sprinkling a form of powder along cracks of the two-inch-thick steel door. He bent down, using a small lighter that he held in his hand.

Doc's lithe spring took him well away from the door

before the intense, white-hot heat started snaking along the door edges. Metal melted before the girl's wide-eyed gaze; the massive door abruptly sagged on its heavy hinges.

"Thermite," Ham explained to Honey Sanders. "Hottest burning substance known. Come on."

Leaving the captives bound and gagged, they returned to the road stand where Doc's limousine had first been parked. Monk and the girl located the two real policemen who had been tied up and left in the woods.

Doc drove them to their local headquarters, explaining about the captives back at the gas tank. The bronze man was assured that plenty of officers would be sent out to take care of the crooks.

Doc made arrangements by which, later, the captives would be sent to his special "college"—to the very institution from which their boss, Birmingham Jones, had escaped.

Doc and his aides, with the girl, drove back to New York. Late afternoon papers were on the streets, and there seemed to be some extras.

Monk got out of the car to buy a paper, stared at the heavy type and quickly brought the paper back to Doc Savage.

"Blazes!" Monk piped. "Just lookit that!"

The item read:

EXPLOSION ROCKS
LONG ISLAND TOWN

SECOND MYSTERIOUS
BLAST TODAY

Bulletin

At a few moments before noon today, at one of the plants of Modern Paints, Inc., located in Long Island City, a terrific blast tore down a section of buildings where hundreds of employees were just ready to leave for their noon lunch hour.

It is believed that the number of dead and missing will reach at least twenty-four people. But at this writing—scarcely a half hour since the accident occurred —it is impossible to say just how many have been killed and seriously injured.

Plant officials cannot explain the mysterious blast. And police have been unable to yet investigate because of fire that has broken out in store rooms adjoining the demolished section of the plant.

Cornelius Duval, millionaire owner of Modern Paints, Inc., refused to talk with reporters. Earlier today, at another of the wealthy manufacturer's plants in New Jersey, another mysterious explosion occurred.

It was not necessary for Doc or the others to read further. Ham whistled.

Long Tom said, "Doc, what do you figure is behind this?"

The bronze man had started the car again, was sending it smoothly and swiftly downtown through late afternoon traffic. For several moments he did not answer the question.

Then he said briefly, "Possibly we have overlooked some angle that involves the section called Sleepy Hollow."

Monk, in the rear seat, jumped.

"Golly, Doc!" he exclaimed. "You mean something about that blasted goblin thing that Honey, here, and I saw?"

Honey Sanders looked questioningly at Doc Savage. The bronze man had been talking to her quietly all during the drive back from New Jersey. His questions had seemed casual; a number of them had pertained to her home life in the region known as Sleepy Hollow.

The girl had thought the questions merely part of an idle conversation. But now she suddenly understood that she had been mistaken.

There was nothing ever casual about this remarkable bronze fellow. There had been a purpose behind his questioning, she abruptly realized.

And this was evident in Doc's next comments.

He said, "Long Tom, you and Monk might go out there to that paint plant and investigate. Ham can wait at headquarters with the girl. If anything develops at Sleepy Hollow, you will hear from me."

A few moments later, he dropped the others off before the skyscraper building containing his eighty-sixth floor headquarters.

Dusk was settling over the Westchester hills when Doc finally left Manhattan behind him and sped along the wide parkway that led toward Tarrytown and the region of Sleepy Hollow.

It was also dark enough that driveway lights should have been turned on in the service station where the long, serious-looking mechanic worked alone.

The man was the same fellow who had tangled with Monk when the scrappy chemist had piled up his car in the service-station driveway.

But the man had apparently forgotten all about turning on lights now. He was strangely excited about something. He raced inside the small building that served as office and service station. He leaped toward a wall phone as though his life depended on it.

A second later he was excitedly talking to the operator.

"Look, get me Doc Savage, in New York! Get me long distance! I've got something to tell Doc Savage! I've got something to tell him about Patrick Valentine—"

The long-looking, serious station owner paused, stammering, "Oh, sure. I forgot! Get me Doc Savage and I'll tell *him* that!"

He waited. Long distance, apparently, knew the number he sought, for shortly a connection was made and a piping voice was saying:

"Hello? This is the headquarters of Doc Savage."

The station man was so excited that words got stuck in his throat for a moment. "Listen!" he finally got out. "It's about Patrick Valentine! Get me Doc Savage! Hurry! I just learned—"

Whatever the long man had learned would forever remain a mystery. And all because, in his excitement, he had forgotten to turn on the station lights.

The darkly clad figure had taken advantage of that

gloom created by the absence of lights. He slipped into the building on soft-soled shoes, moved up behind the tall man talking excitedly at the phone. The knife which he used made a slight crunching sound as it slid between ribs in the station owner's back.

The shadowy figure stepped back, the knife still gripped firmly in his hand. He watched the tall fellow fall, kick a few times, and then lay still.

Then the prowler moved to a workbench, wiped the knife blade off on a greasy piece of waste.

A sputtering, firecracker sound was coming from the dangling receiver of the wall phone. The killer stepped back, replaced the receiver on the hook. It was impossible to see the man's face in the darkness.

But he seemed sure of his movements. He appeared not to hurry. Before leaving, he stepped to a desk that was obviously the only "office" the station boasted. He fumbled around with papers on the desk.

Going out, he closed the doors behind him. The doors contained spring locks, and now, to all appearances—seeing that no lights had been turned on—the place was closed up.

The prowler slipped off into the night.

On the nearby Post Road, a car passed occasionally. It was the time of night when most nearby residents were at dinner.

Crickets started their night chatter in the adjacent woods behind the darkened building.

The long, expensive-looking limousine rolled into the station about twenty minutes later. The driver did not get out of the car. But his sharp eyes took in the racks of oil still placed on the gas-pump "island" outside the station.

He saw other indications which made it seem queer the place should be locked up for the night—while supplies still remained outside.

The man at the wheel of the big car was Doc Savage.

Doc did not climb out of the car. Instead, he started up, rolled out of the station and, a few moments later, sent the car down through one of the many shaded lanes that were a part of peaceful-looking Sleepy Hollow.

Ten minutes later, none would have recognized the bronze man as he returned, on foot, to the darkened service station.

For Doc walked with a stoop. His clothes were ragged. His remarkable bronze features and hair were concealed by a grimy-looking make-up substance that gave him the appearance of a hobo just off a freight train. His hair and skin were now dark.

Doc gained admittance to the station through a rear window. Seconds later, he was examining the stabbed man.

The bronze man used a small flashlight which he carefully shielded with his hands. He looked for signs of prints that might have been left by the murderer. There were none.

Doc noted the dead man's position by the wall telephone. He lifted the receiver, got the operator, then was asking quietly, "What was the last call made from this number?"

"Just a moment, please," said the girl.

Then Doc was informed that a call had been put through to New York. His own headquarters phone number was repeated.

If the bronze man was surprised, the fact was not expressed in his voice.

"Please get that number again," he requested.

Monk answered the call.

"Doc!" the chemist exclaimed when he heard the bronze man's voice. "Look, Doc, some fella just called you a little while ago. He was all het up about this man named Patrick Valentine. I sorta figure he knew where we might locate Valentine—"

"Then," Doc put it, "that explains why this man here was killed."

"Killed? Who?" Monk wanted to know.

Briefly, Doc told about the dead service-station operator; that he was calling from near Sleepy Hollow.

Monk got excited. "That explains why he was cut

off. Doc! That's all he had time to say—something about knowing this Valentine guy. He must 'a' learned something."

"Yes," Doc Savage said. "Perhaps, by morning, we will know the answer. If you do not hear from me by then, you'd better investigate."

The bronze man hung up.

He spent a few more moments going carefully over the inside of the building. On top of some scattered papers on the desk, he saw the penciled circle drawn around the brief news item.

The paper was one published locally, and the item was just another bit of gossip in a column devoted to local chatter.

It read:

> The *Nancy Lee*, former river showboat that has been tied up at Kelly's Landing for the past two years, is reported sold to an out-of-town junk dealer. Report is that the decaying old schooner will shortly be towed away.

A frown momentarily touched the bronze man's brow as he swiftly read the item by aid of the shielded flashlight ray. Odd that a garage man would be interested in such news!

And stranger still that the words "Doc Savage" should be scrawled across the page, just beneath the news item!

There was enough indication of greasy finger marks around the scrawled notation to show that the dead service-station man had written Doc's name.

Before slipping out the rear window, Doc Savage called the operator again and said, "Send the police at once to the Highway Service Station on the Albany Post Road."

Under the covering gloom of night, he returned quickly to his car.

The *Nancy Lee* sat low enough in the water to suggest that her seams were cracking open and that her hold must be half filled with water. Her rigging had long since been removed.

Doc Savage had had no trouble in locating the old showboat. Up until two years ago, on summer nights, a New York boat line had featured nightly trips up the river to where the *Nancy Lee* was anchored. A stock company had put on popular old revivals aboard the schooner.

Since the fad had died out, the schooner had been tied up long enough along the river front to make it almost a landmark.

The long wharf was as aged-looking as the boat itself. Decayed planking sagged beneath the bronze man's shoes as he made his way along the stringpiece.

At the end of the wharf, in the deceptive darkness, he located a battered gangplank that led up to the bulking sides of the clumsy-looking craft.

He went aboard.

On deck, Doc stood listening. Then, carefully, he made his way along the deck.

Silence lay heavy everywhere. The moon had not yet come up, and the night was dark.

But the bronze man had no trouble finding his way about. His remarkable eyesight guided him accurately. There was no indication that this old tub had been used in months.

He went below, located a passageway that led forward. It was necessary to use a flashlight down here. A coal-black cat scurried up a companionway ahead.

Doc paused before an open doorway, looked into what had once been the skipper's cabin.

Dishes with scraps of food upon them were set upon a table in the room!

Cautiously, Doc Savage moved inside the room.

Something slammed above him, out in the passageway. It was followed by another thumping sound farther aft. It was abruptly darker outside the room.

Only one thing could have happened. Hatches above had been slammed shut!

Doc Savage whirled, to leap outside the room.

But the door jerked shut, men tumbled out of dark

corners all around him. A light flashed on in the room, the ray of a powerful hand-flash.

Guns and faces that were not pleasant hemmed in the bronze giant.

A harsh voice said, "Wait'll Birmingham Jones hears what we got for him!"

Chapter X

THE *NANCY LEE*

The man who spoke made one mistake when he addressed Doc Savage. He came a step within the circle of grim-jawed gunmen.

The bronze man moved.

Or rather—to those who were momentarily amazed —there was a flash of blurred motion and the crook who had spoken was down on the cabin deck. He had been knocked senseless.

Holding their fire for fear of hitting their own men, the mob closed in on the bronze giant.

They were thrown aside like bouncing tenpins. Heads cracked the cabin walls. There was suddenly a great deal of swearing and struggling and confusion.

Doc Savage managed to knock half a dozen big thugs into unconscious heaps before, through sheer force of numbers, he was dragged to the deck.

For at sounds of the battle, other tough-looking hombres had come running into the cabin. The jam got so thick that they were hitting each other. There must have been two dozen assailants now in the room.

They got the bronze fellow tied up. As though this wasn't enough, someone carried in two blankets and the heavy material was ripped into long strips.

Around the ropes that already held the bronze man motionless, the strips of blanket were wound until Doc looked like a helpless mummy. Only his face was revealed.

Even then, the men stood well back from where Doc was laid out, like a long round log, on the deck.

One individual—a swarthy fellow with features ugly with old scars—said warningly, "Keep your eyes on him! I wouldn't feel safe near this Doc Savage guy even if he was tied with anchor chain!"

"O. K., Pinky," someone said to the man with the scarred face.

For Pinky was one of the two men who had been at the "college" upstate. He stood back now, watching the bronze giant's prone figure carefully, and he seemed to be waiting for something.

Most of the group fell silent, except for those who were picking themselves up from the deck, rubbing bruised jaws as they did so.

A thug asked, "What next, Pinky?"

"Keep your shirt on," said Pinky. "He'll be here soon. But you don't think he's dumb enough to come aboard while we're tied up here, do you? He'll meet us out in the river."

Even as Pinky spoke, there was a slight motion of the old schooner. Not the motion caused by the throb or pumping of engines, but a smooth gliding sensation as though the craft was being towed.

The gliding feel of the boat continued for about half an hour. Then it stopped. There was a clattering racket as, apparently, an anchor was lowered.

Doc Savage had not moved. Only his eyes remained stirring and restless, as they touched upon individuals grouped above him. Something about those unusual flake-gold eyes caused the others to remain clear—though it was obvious that the bronze figure could not move an inch.

There came the sounds of feet moving on the deck above, and then men were pounding down the companion and along the passageway outside the room.

Two burly men barged into the room. They stepped

aside and the man they had preceded was revealed.

He was well dressed, tall, slender and dark. He hardly looked like a gangster or crook.

But his eyes were a deadly gray. Also, they had sort of a vacant stare.

He indicated the trussed-up figure of the bronze man and asked, "Who's the mug?"

"That's Doc Savage," informed Pinky.

"Who?"

"Look, Birmingham," Pinky explained carefully, "Doc Savage is the guy the big boy wanted us to capture, remember? Doc Savage and any of his assistants who are working with him."

"Oh!" said dark-haired Birmingham Jones, but he did not seem unduly impressed.

Pinky explained further. "Look, Birmingham, Doc Savage"—he jabbed a finger at the form tied up on the floor—"this guy is the mug who had you sent to that place upstate. To the college, remember?"

It seemed to take a moment for that to sink into Birmingham Jones' brain. Then he stiffened. A peculiar glint came into his fishy eyes. His hand moved beneath his coat.

"Then I'll kill him!" said Birmingham Jones flatly.

Only for the fact that quick-moving Pinky seized the well-dressed man's hand, was Doc Savage saved from a speedy death.

Exasperated, Pinky tried to explain to Birmingham Jones.

"Now listen," he rapped. "You've been doing all right. The boss thinks you're good. But we're not to rub out the bronze guy—yet!"

Birmingham Jones shrugged. "Why not?"

"Because we gotta use him to get those assistants of his here, too—aboard the boat. We're shoving out at midnight, and the big boy has ideas how he's gonna wipe out this Doc Savage crowd all at once. At sea!"

"Oh!" said Birmingham Jones again absently, and Pinky gave the man a frown.

Then, after a moment, Birmingham Jones asked, "But how you gonna get them guys up here?"

"Watch!" said Pinky, and he made a motion to the waiting mob. "Bring along the bronze guy!"

It took six men to pick up the bronze man. He was carried through a passageway for about half the length of the old schooner. There was some trouble in getting him down a narrow ladder to another deck below.

Then Doc was carried into a long, brilliantly lighted room that was like nothing that had ever been on a rotting sailing ship.

The room was obviously a laboratory. There was the soft hum of a power unit that was apparently used to develop electricity. Devices, machinery installed in the room, said that someone here knew a whole lot about science.

Scar-faced Pinky caught the thoughtful regard in the bronze man's eyes and grinned.

"Some set-up, eh, guy?" he queried. "A whole lot of people around Sleepy Hollow would lose their uppers if they ever guessed about this *Nancy Lee* tub!"

Doc's eyes flickered.

A rack of huge cylinders at one side of the long room caught his eye. His glance touched the objects so briefly that none had seen the recognition which was mirrored in the bronze figure's eyes.

Doc was suddenly being lifted and carried again. Pinky directed the group toward a table where various radio equipment was set up.

Birmingham Jones came along also, and it was notable that everyone paid him the deepest respect. For though they were hardened crooks, each man appeared to have a slight fear of this tall, pale-eyed, well-dressed man.

"Oh, I get it!" Birmingham Jones suddenly put in. "Valentine said we could force Doc Savage to lead his other men up here. You're going to use the radio?"

Pinky paused, turning away from the dials which he had been manipulating.

"Birmingham," he said, "you're improving! You just

keep remembering the boss' orders, and you'll be the biggest public enemy in the world today!"

Doc had been placed on his feet, his handlers grunting as they held his great figure upright. The bronze man's sharp eyes caught the wave length at which Pinky had set the short-wave set.

It was a wave length used by Doc and his men whenever they wished to communicate with each other.

Pinky, at a nod from Birmingham Jones, was suddenly directing, "O.K., Savage. You'd better make it good. Whoever answers from your New York headquarters, you tell 'em you got everything figured out up here at Sleepy Hollow. Tell 'em all to get up here right away. Tell those birds you'll meet them at the bridge on the Post Road, just a mile south of that service station where you were tonight."

The short-wave set was already humming. In a moment, contact would be made with the bronze man's headquarters.

For the first time, Doc Savage spoke.

He said quietly, "It's too bad you have gone to this useless trouble."

Pinky's lips twisted into a snarl.

"Talk to them, damn you!" he snapped.

The bronze giant's lips were clamped shut. His eyes were steady and burning.

Birmingham Jones stepped forward. "Allow me, gentlemen," he said.

The gun appeared miraculously in his hand and its barrel raked down across the bronze man's metallic features.

Later, after using the gun barrel several more times, even Birmingham Jones stared. Everyone looked at the mummified figure.

Doc Savage's features, his expression was as inscrutable as an image made of bronze.

But he started to sweat. The blanket strips wound securely around his remarkable body became wet. Beads of perspiration rolled off Doc's high forehead.

Those holding the wrapped figure upright found their hands slippery with the moisture.

Pinky, though, was paying no attention. He suddenly exclaimed as he tuned in the transmitting set, "Hell with him! Watch this!"

He made a motion indicating that Doc Savage was to be removed out of speaking distance of the transmitter. The hum of the short-wave set became louder, and then Pinky was abruptly saying into a microphone:

"Hello, Monk. This is Doc Savage speaking—"

Pinky's voice was remarkably like the bronze man's own.

Chapter XI

TIP-OFF!

The scene was the reception room of Doc Savage's skyscraper headquarters. Outside the windows, far below, the million and one lights of Manhattan at night shone like bright small stars.

Monk came through a doorway. His face split in a broad smile at the vision of loveliness in the person of slender, attractive Honey Sanders. But he glared at Ham, clad in a new suit, and carrying on an easy conversation with the girl. There might have been a fight between the pals right then, but at the moment Long Tom entered Doc's headquarters from the outside entrance hallway. He looked excited.

Ham asked, "What did you find out about Cornelius Duval? Did you manage to see that millionaire yet?"

Long Tom shook his head. "No. But I found out something else."

"What?"

"That Duval has a private estate up there in the Westchester hills behind Sleepy Hollow. Seeing as how a whole lot of the trouble started there, bet you he's mixed up in this thing!"

The girl's deep-blue eyes widened. "I never heard of Mr. Duval living anywhere around Sleepy Hollow," she put in.

Long Tom nodded. "He didn't. Seems he's just bought this estate lately. Hardly anyone knows about it yet. One of his secretaries told me about it."

The girl said, "But why, *if* Duval is involved in this mystery, would he have some of his own plants blown up?"

Ham had a ready answer for that one. "Smoke screen," he offered. "To throw suspicion off himself."

The flickering of a small red bulb high on a wall in the room drew everyone's attention. It was Long Tom who stepped quickly toward the laboratory doorway, to enter that part of Doc Savage's headquarters which contained much of his delicate and intricate electrical and radio equipment.

A moment later he called out to the others, "It's the short wave. Maybe a message from Doc!"

Ham and Monk, with the girl, moved quickly toward the lab.

A section of the huge room was given over to radio apparatus that would have brought words of praise from broadcasting and control-room engineers.

Long Tom was manipulating the various dials on a huge receiving unit. A moment later, the voice of Doc Savage came from a loud-speaker overhead.

It was the message that the scarred-faced crook called Pinky, imitating Doc's voice from the old show-boat up the Hudson, was putting on the air.

They all heard the urgent words, listened to the directions ordering them to meet the bronze man at the bridge on the Post Road near Sleepy Hollow.

Monk looked delighted. "Blazes! Let's get going!" he said.

Doc Savage was just signing off. It was Ham who suddenly exclaimed, "Listen!"

They all heard the soft, unmistakable trilling sound of the bronze man while Doc was still talking.

Long Tom stared. "Trick!" the electrical expert rapped.

Ham nodded. "Doc couldn't make the sound and talk, too! Someone else was talking in his place—but Doc must 'a' been somewhere near there and made the trilling, so we'd know!"

The trilling sound of the bronze man was a form of ventriloquism. It could be created by Doc Savage without anyone close by being aware of its source.

Monk summed up the situation.

"Daggonit!" he exploded. "Doc's in trouble!"

It was decided to leave Long Tom with the girl, at headquarters. The electrical expert had one word of caution to give, however, before Ham and Monk, this time accompanied by the pets, departed.

"It appears," said Long Tom, "that the message came from some boat located up the river. That part about meeting Doc at the highway bridge was probably a trap. You might watch for a boat somewhere in the vicinity of Sleepy Hollow."

Long Tom's deductions were more than likely fairly accurate, for he had carefully charted, using a direction-finder that was ultrasensitive up to a radius of fifty miles, the source of the radio waves. Using intricate charts devised by the bronze man himself, Long Tom was thus able to give the two aides a lead.

Fifteen minutes later, Ham and Monk were taking off from Doc Savage's water-front hangar in one of the fast speed planes.

The thing floating in the water looked like a matchstick that bulged slightly in the middle.

That is, from their position several thousand feet above, it looked so. But Ham knew it must be the schooner they sought, for it was the only craft visible for miles in the now moonlight night.

Monk, at the controls, had been flying the fast plane so high that no sound of its motors could possibly reach anyone who might be watching from the river.

"All right," Ham directed, "cut the engines and go down. Better land close in to shore. We can swim out, and that way we won't be spotted."

Monk, worried about Doc Savage, and anxious to get to his aid, stuck the nose of the plane down and let the ship dive.

Ham let out a yell.

"Fool!" Ham rapped. "You want to yank the wings off this ship?"

Monk pulled out of the steep dive, threw the plane into a more smooth spiral.

He said calmly, "I'm in a hurry."

They landed without mishap, much to the dapper lawyer's amazement.

Monk made use of the river current to let the small amphibian drift in beneath tree branches that overshadowed the river bank. Making the plane secure, Monk yanked off his coat and climbed out on a wing.

"Let's get going!" he squeaked impatiently.

Ham didn't like the idea of soaking his newest suit, but approach to the old schooner lying out in the river must be made in this manner.

The two aides slid into the warm water and struck out for the darkened ship.

Once, Monk commented, "Betcha we've made a mistake. That old tub looks like she's gonna sink any minute."

"Keep quiet!" Ham snapped.

For the bulky lines of the old sailing ship were not far ahead, and sound traveled easily across the calm water in the quiet night.

Ten minutes later Ham and Monk were swimming silently beneath the scabby sides of the schooner. They worked their way toward the bow, where there was some amount of shadow.

Monk, with the agility of an ape, went hand over hand up the taut anchor chain. Ham followed. Silently, both men swung up on deck.

Not a dozen feet from them, the man was seated on the coil of heavy rope. His chin kept going down and touching his chest. He was apparently asleep.

Monk moved quietly toward a rack where old belaying pins were still in place. He removed one, came back to Ham, grinned, then swung the heavy object.

The man—he had obviously been stationed here to do guard duty—went into a more sound sleep.

Monk hefted the belaying pin. "Maybe we'll find some more of these mugs," he said hopefully.

"Quiet!" Ham rapped. He led the way forward.

They covered the entire deck, located no more lookouts. They started below, through the only hatch opening that they could find unlocked.

Monk whispered in his squeaky voice, "Blazes! Maybe that guy back there only lives alone on this tub. Bet Long Tom was wrong about it being a boat where they got Doc—"

Ham hissed, "Shut up! This might be a trap—"

It was!

Men boiled out of assorted hiding places and slammed into Ham and Monk, in the dark, narrow passageway below decks.

Monk bellowed, using the belaying pin in the close, shadowy quarters. Ham was using his quick-moving fists.

The fight, a tangled, snarling, cursing knot, swayed up and down the passage.

Monk wasn't particular how he used the heavy weapon which he gripped in a hairy fist. Men went down like slugged cattle. Others climbed over their fallen comrades and tried to reach the battling chemist. Ham picked others off with his deft blows.

But the two aides were slowly backed toward the open, lighted doorway. It was the well-equipped laboratory that had been installed below decks in the apparently worthless schooner.

Monk backed into the room, grinning when he saw that there was more space in which he could now swing the club.

"Yeo-o-ow!" the chemist bawled. "Now bring 'em on!"

Behind Monk and his partner, a cool voice said, "That's about enough of that!"

Monk and Ham spun around to stare at the automatics held in the scar-faced man's steady fists.

Pinky, the one holding the guns, grinned. "We kinda had a hunch the bronze guy tipped you punks off!" he said.

Chapter XII

CROOKS MOVE OUT!

While Pinky kept the two Doc Savage men covered, they were swiftly grabbed from behind and tied with heavy, stout cords.

It was then that Monk saw the bronze man.

"Doc!" he cried worriedly.

Ham, too, from his helpless position on the floor, stared.

Both aides saw the mummylike figure propped up against a bulkhead.

Doc Savage's metallic features—the only part of him visible above the tightly wrapped bindings—showed the streaks of redness where a gun barrel had left its wicked marks.

Across Doc's lips had been placed adhesive tape, so that he had been unable to warn Monk and Ham.

Pinky put away his automatics and nodded approvingly to his assistants.

"We didn't get all of Doc Savage's men, but this helps. There's one still down in New York with the girl. The other two aides, we've heard, are somewhere in Europe. I think Birmingham's planning on taking care of the girl and the one they call Long Tom on the way through New York tonight."

At the question in Ham's sharp eyes, Pinky grinned and went on:

"Too bad we can't stay around to see the fun, guy. But we're shovin' off. See you all in hell some day!"

Scar-faced Pinky looked back at his henchmen. "You sure you got everything off this tub that was needed? Valentine'll raise plenty of hell if you didn't. An' we can't come back."

One of the burly thugs nodded. "Yeah. We got it all." He grinned as he stared at the helpless Doc Savage captives. 'Damn right we won't be back. Back to *what?*"

The others laughed also. It seemed to be a huge joke.

Still grinning at Monk and Ham, lying helplessly trussed up on the floor, the men started filing out of the laboratory room. Pinky flung a last glance at Doc Savage, propped up against the bulkhead.

"Yeah," he repeated, "see you all in hell!"

He, too, went out; and a moment later the faint sound of feet tramping across the decks above could be heard. Silence shortly dropped down, down like a wraith over the schooner.

Monk tried to twist around. He saw Doc Savage, as helpless as a wrapped-up mummy. He twisted far enough to stare at Ham, likewise unable to move.

Monk said, "What the blazes did those guys mean about seein' us in hell?"

Ham looked worried. "I'm trying not to think about it," he said, twisting and squirming in a hopeless attempt to get free of the ropes.

Both looked up at Doc Savage. Both saw the perspiration-soaked cloth strips that were wrapped securely around the bronze man. Doc was moist enough to have been dipped in water.

And both aides started when those wet bindings suddenly split wide apart and Doc Savage, as remarkably alert as ever, stepped free of them.

It was as though acid had eaten through ropes and blanket strips, rotting them as though they might have been tissue paper.

Doc quickly yanked the adhesive from his mouth and

said, "They have probably gone far enough now that we can trail them without being seen."

Doc turned to his two aides, started on the ropes that held them. Within seconds Monk and Ham were on their feet, with the hairy chemist asking questions.

"Doc, what happened—" Monk started.

"No time for explanations," Doc Savage rapped swiftly. "Thing is to get off this boat. Hurry!"

The bronze man motioned them toward the passageway, urged them to hurry as they headed for the upper deck.

The upper deck was deserted. Monk stared around.

"They must 'a' got away in a boat," he piped. He started looking around to see if there was a boat they themselves could use.

But Doc said tensely, "No time for that. Overside! Quick!"

Ham paused only long enough to indicate, approximately, where the plane was hidden along the shore, then leaped overside with Monk and Ham.

A couple of moments later, Monk was gasping as a result of the terrific speed the bronze man was setting with his powerful overhand strokes through the water.

"Blazes, Doc!" Monk howled. "What's the rush?"

Doc did not let up in his pace. His voice came clearly over his shoulder.

"You have," he warned, "just about two more minutes to save yourself from death."

That was enough to make Monk splash through the water like an Ohio River side-wheeler. Ham followed suit.

Even as, half winded, both aides were dragging themselves up on shore, they heard the peculiar, shrill whistling sound out over the river.

Monk stood up, yelled, "Goshamighty! There it is! That flying hobgoblin of a thing. Lookit, will ya! It's gonna—"

Doc snapped, "Down! Down on your stomachs!"

The terrific concussion came a split second later. The blast was enough to spray sand from the small strip of beach over the three prone figures.

Out in the river, the old schooner—the *Nancy Lee* —went up in the air as though it might have been a toy jerked by a string.

Later, in the plane, and as they scoured the river front for moving small boats, and the nearby side roads for any signs of fast-moving cars, Doc made brief explanations.

First, he explained his own delay at releasing himself from the mummylike bindings.

"It was uncertain for a while whether Birmingham Jones would return to the schooner or not. There is a probability that he went to meet the one known as Valentine."

Ham understood. "And you hoped, by pretending you were still helpless, to see the guy who is really behind the mystery?"

The bronze man, at the controls of the plane, nodded.

Monk interjected, "But goshamighty, Doc? How did you loosen those blasted ropes and things?"

Doc indicated his still moist hands. "A penetrating fluid which was in a vial in my coat pocket. It eats into anything except human flesh. Managed to squeeze the vial and break it while they were tying me up. The stuff spreads like kerosene."

"Then," Monk said, "you were just fooling those mugs so you could get a line on the real Valentine?"

Doc was flying low now, intently scanning the shore line beneath them. He swung the plane and returned upriver again.

"Yes," he admitted in response to Monk's question. "But they changed their plans after Birmingham Jones got in touch with them by radio."

"What do you mean?" Ham queried.

"Valentine, wherever he was, had ordered the schooner destroyed. He needed it no longer."

Monk stared. "You mean that flying whatchacallit thing destroyed it, Doc?"

"Apparently."

"But heck! If this guy Valentine wasn't even *there,* then how could he—"

Doc said, "That's only one of our problems. The question is: Where is Valentine and what is he really trying to do?"

"Yeah," agreed the hairy chemist.

So far, they had found no trace of those who had escaped from the schooner.

And so Doc Savage put the plane down at a point near where he had left his car hidden on the east shore of the Hudson. Monk was directed to drive the car back to headquarters and to meet Doc and Ham there.

On the flight downriver again, Ham asked the bronze man, "That laboratory aboard the schooner, Doc—it had something to do with Valentine and what he is up to?"

"Yes. But now he is through with it. Obviously, it was only an experimental workshop. That's why the schooner was blown up. Valentine is making a quick move to some other point. It looks as though he is now ready for some grand coup."

Doc's unusual eyes were thoughtful.

"It might," he added, "be a good idea to see Long Tom. He started to say something this afternoon about a thing he noticed at the Duval plant in New Jersey. But there has been no time yet to question him."

And so Doc Savage was silent during the remainder of the short flight into New York.

They arrived back at Doc's skyscraper headquarters about midnight. Ham hurried ahead into the reception room, anxious about Honey Sanders.

Doc Savage was more interested, at the moment, in talking to Long Tom.

But Ham and the bronze giant were not going to talk to anyone.

The electrical wizard and the girl were not in the library, reception room or lab.

They had vanished.

Chapter XIII

DEATH FLIES HIGH

At one that morning, there had still been no word from Long Tom or the girl.

At one thirty, Monk returned from Sleepy Hollow with the bronze man's car. The chemist hurried into headquarters with excitement in his little eyes.

"You know what?" he piped.

Ham gave his partner a sour look. "I suppose you've got into a jam again!" he suggested coolly.

"Listen!" Monk hurried on, ignoring the dapper lawyer's remark. "I did a little investigatin' up there at Sleepy Hollow before starting back. And I found out something."

"Well, *what*, stupid?" Ham demanded.

"That Duval millionaire guy has pulled a sneak," informed Monk. "He's flown the coop, walked out!"

Doc Savage looked interested. "Just what do you mean?" he prodded.

Monk exploded, "Blazes, Doc, Duval has gone to Europe! Took a Clipper plane! Now why do you suppose he's gone and done that?"

The bronze man said nothing for a moment. Then he remarked, "Possibly Duval's departure explains the sudden disappearance of Birmingham Jones and the others."

Monk immediately jumped to a conclusion.

"You mean, Doc," he queried, "Duval is behind this danged mystery?"

Doc Savage was moving toward the phone. "Not exactly," he said. "But it might be interesting to learn about other plane movements tonight."

Monk looked puzzled. Ham was intently listening as the bronze man started making phone calls and asking pertinent questions.

It appeared that Doc was calling the leading airports around greater New York. He was questioning officials about any planes that had departed for Europe or South American countries.

Doc spent considerable time covering every known flying field and sea base.

Finally he hung up and said quietly, "Three Clipper planes left for Europe tonight. Each was crowded with passengers, and none of them were women. It might be interesting to know who were aboard those planes.

"Did you get any names?" Monk asked.

"Yes, but they could be pseudonyms." Doc mentioned the name of an airport that ran regular flights abroad. "The dispatcher there said it was the largest order they'd ever filled for passage to Europe."

"What do you make of it, Doc?" Ham wanted to know.

"Wait," the bronze man said, and stepped toward his laboratory.

Ham and Monk followed. Doc was manipulating the dials of a powerful radio transmitting set.

He explained, "Renny and Johnny are in Paris. They were to stand by for a message from headquarters at seven this morning. It is just about that over there now."

For some time, the bronze man worked with the dials of the powerful set. When tubes were warmed up and things seemed to be adjusted to his satisfaction, he said into a microphone:

"Doc Savage calling Colonel John Renwick—"

The bronze man repeated the words several times.

Finally, an answer came over the loud-speaker located over the apparatus-filled table.

"Renny speaking," a booming voice said. *"Is that you, Doc?"*

Doc Savage started to explain about the series of

mysterious circumstances that had occurred near New York. He told about Duval, and of the man named Birmingham Jones.

Doc said, "Birmingham Jones, apparently, is working for someone with a diabolical scheme to create destruction and horror, Renny."

"What does Doc mean?" Monk said to Ham, as both aides listened.

"Keep quiet," the lawyer rapped.

Doc was saying, "Are you still tuned in, Renny?"

There was an abrupt, slight frown on the bronze man's usually placid features. He twisted the dials quickly, spoke again.

A peculiar crackling sound came from the loud-speaker, and behind the sound Renny's booming was heard to gradually fade.

Doc looked tense about something. The static sound increased, grew louder in the set.

Abruptly he whirled away from the radio apparatus, ordered, "Ham! Get on that direction-finder unit. Hurry! And Monk! Turn on the sound-detector!"

The stocky chemist, puzzled, jumped to obey.

Doc Savage called out positions to which the apparatus was to be set. Both units, he requested, were to be trained on locations that would indicate the Atlantic!

The static sound in the loud-speaker was getting worse. There was no trace of Renny's voice at all.

Doc suddenly turned off the short-wave, moved swiftly to the instruments that Ham and Monk were adjusting. Doc took charge.

For several moments, he made fine adjustments with the sensitized, delicate devices. Once he commented, "It appears to be closer now."

Ham, watching and listening to noises that came from the sound detector, asked, "What's coming closer —a plane, Doc?"

"No, the flying thing."

Monk jumped.

The chemist saw that the bronze giant was using

several delicate instruments now. Some of them of Doc Savage's own invention, Monk knew that these detectors were uncanny in their accuracy. They could tell exact location of anything in the air up to a radius of several hundred miles.

Doc had suddenly spun away from the detector devices.

"Quick!" he ordered. "The ray machine. Set it in position!"

Monk, the chemist in the bronze man's organization, was beginning to gain an inkling of the truth.

"Doc!" he howled. "You mean some sort of thing is gonna attack us—*here?*"

The bronze giant nodded briefly.

"The position of the thing is approximately fifty miles out to sea. It will reach here within moments now."

"Within *moments?*" Monk gulped, completely flabbergasted.

But Doc Savage was already flinging open especially constructed, huge windows in one wall of the big laboratory. The space opened to the night was all of a dozen feet wide, and gave a panoramic view of lower New York Bay, a part of Long Island. Beyond, was the Atlantic.

Doc whirled back to help Ham wheel a huge machine toward the wall opening. The thing looked like the kind of powerful searchlight used by army engineers in aërial bombardment maneuvers.

But when Doc Savage turned on the machine, no light came from its front. The machine was an invisible-ray device made to repel certain kinds of forces.

The bronze man made certain other adjustments, stepped back to the direction-finder.

He said tensely, "The ray should hit the flying thing within the next moment. If it doesn't—"

Doc let the words trail off, moved to a position where he could watch through the window opening.

The tone of his voice had indicated that if his calculations were wrong, then they were all doomed for some kind of destruction.

It was Monk who suddenly squealed, *"Look!"*

The best description of the phenomenon might be to state that a comet had exploded. There was a trail of sparks through the night sky as something smashed to fiery bits high in the air.

And as the weird, distant explosion took place, the bronze man seemed to relax slightly.

"Another moment," he commented, "and it would have been here." There was perspiration standing out on the bronze giant's metallic features.

"But, Doc—" Monk started, full of questions.

The ringing of the phone in the library interrupted them. Ham hurried to answer it.

He was back almost instantly, his face strained and tense.

"It was the girl—Honey Sanders!" he exclaimed. "And—"

"She ask for me?" Monk got in, hopefully.

"—and it's about Long Tom!" Ham finished.

"Long Tom?" Doc caught the urgency in Ham's words.

"Long Tom is at our water-front hangar. He's trying to hold off the guys who are trying to destroy our equipment and planes stored there!"

Monk let out a yell of rage. He was already leaping toward the door. Ham hesitated only long enough to hear the bronze man's comment:

"Leave the ray machine turned on. It is hardly probable that there will be another aërial attack, but it might be wise to guard against one."

Doc hurried with his two aides toward an express elevator that would drop them swiftly to the basement of the skyscraper.

The "flea run" was the name Monk had once given to the high-speed, pneumatic-tube device that was almost an instantaneous method of transportation from Doc's headquarters to the water-front hangar.

A small, compact cage carried the three men underground through a specially constructed tube. A cushion of air finally stopped the hurtling car with breathtaking suddenness.

Monk gasped, "Some day this blasted thing is gonna yank my head right off my shoulders!"

Climbing out, Ham said sarcastically, "That'll be the day!"

Doc Savage said, "It looks like we're too late."

They were in a huge, vaulted space that contained several planes. These ranged from a vast, trimotored ship to various types of small speed planes and autogiros. Every ship was an amphibian—capable of descending on land or water.

The warehouse floor sloped downward—to a wide apron of cement that dropped off into the Hudson River, adjacent. The hangar doors were open and there seemed to be a whole lot of excitement going on outside.

Doc, Monk and Ham raced across the vast hangar floor. But even as they ran, they heard the powerful roar of a ship that was taking off from the river. The mammoth plane rose into the air, circled, started picking up altitude. There came a rattle like the sound of hard peas striking the hangar roof.

Monk leaped to a spot of safety, followed by Ham.

The chemist yelled, "Blazes! Someone's shootin' from that damned plane!"

Doc, meanwhile, had reached the side of skinny Long Tom, crouched down in a grease pit off to the side of the hangar runways.

The electrical wizard had been pumping away with one of the machine pistols that Doc's men always carried. But he straightened now, swore, and started climbing out of the pit.

"Damn!" Long Tom snorted. "They've got away." He looked back into the pit, added, "All right, you two guys. It's safe to climb out now."

Monk stared as the first man came up out of the pit.

It was the stocky, ruddy-faced little constable—Sandy Gower. The evil-smelling pipe was clenched between his teeth, but he was so upset that it had gone out.

"Tarnation!" Sandy Gower fumed. "Paid twenty-five cents for this necktie, and now look at it!"

The flame-orange-colored necktie was grease-spotted as a result of his being in the pit.

Monk stared as he recognized the one who had ordered him temporarily held in jail. He gave Sandy Gower a sour grimace.

"You got stuck nineteen cents then," Monk piped, frowning at the sight of the loud necktie.

Another man came out of the grease pit. He was young, red-haired, not bad-looking. He stared around worriedly.

"Where's Honey?" the young man asked.

It was Long Tom who made explanations.

"This," he said, indicating the red-haired young man, "is Tod Smith, friend of the girl's." The electrical wizard jerked a skinny thumb at Sandy Gower. "So is the constable, here. They came to headquarters looking for her tonight after you left."

"Where's Honey?" repeated Tod Smith worriedly.

Long Tom said, "In the office, where she went to call Doc, here, and the others."

Tod Smith hurried over toward a small office that was in a corner of the large hangar building.

Monk looked after the red-headed young man quizzically. Ham caught the worried regard.

"That," the lawyer stated, "let's you out!"

It appeared that young Tod Smith was the girl's boyfriend.

As Sandy Gower explained, "We've both known Honey for some time. And, me, I'm down here and I'm gonna stick with her—to be her bodyguard from now on!"

Monk suddenly snorted. "Bodyguard? Damned lot of good you were doin' Long Tom by *hiding* down in that pit when he was tryin' to wing that escaping plane!"

Sandy Gower came over to Monk and said loudly, "Listen, here, ape! I still got that jail upriver!"

Monk's fists knotted. "Wanna make something of it?" the chemist demanded.

Doc Savage's voice put a temporary halt to the impending battle.

"What happened?" he asked, looking at Long Tom.

The skinny aide said worriedly, "We were up to headquarters when that black-light burglar alarm set off the signal at the lab. We hustled down here and surprised these mugs, who were all ready to bust up a lot of our equipment."

"But the blasted crooks got away!" Long Tom continued. "And you know, Doc, they had one of those big Clipper transatlantic planes. The pilot, radioman and navigation officer on that plane were being forced to fly the thing by those jaspers!"

Doc prodded quietly, "You have any idea who was in charge of the mob?"

Long Tom nodded, his pale eyes bright.

"Yes. They called him Birmingham Jones!"

Chapter XIV

MYSTERY AT SEA

At noon that same day, the fastest transatlantic vessel afloat moved slowly out of New York harbor and down through the Narrows, out toward the open sea.

Doc Savage's aides—Monk, Ham and Long Tom—were aboard. As were Honey, Sandy Gower and red-headed Tod Smith.

Honey Sanders insisted that, since she was mixed up in this mystery, she was going to see it through.

Young Tod Smith stated that he was not going to let the girl out of his sight. Thus he went along.

And Sandy Gower, grimly determined, went also, to watch over them both—though he bought a ticket in steerage.

Things had developed rapidly through the night, and when Doc Savage had mentioned that the strange menace had moved across the Atlantic, it was Sandy Gower who pointed out that a liner was due to sail that day.

Because of a war situation abroad, liners were only sailing about once a week now.

First, there had been the message from Renny. Contact had finally been made with the engineer in Doc Savage's organization.

Renny told of a strange thing that had occurred early that day in Paris. Some weird sort of explosion had destroyed one of the city's greatest cathedrals.

"Bomb?" Renny had been asked by radio.

"Well, no—not exactly," the engineer had explained. "More like one of those 75 millimeter shells they used during the World War. Only there was something damned funny about it."

"Funny?" Doc had queried.

"Yes. A whole lot of people heard it pass over Paris and the suburbs. A funny, whining sort of thing in the sky. And it didn't come from any war area, Doc! From all reports, it came from the Atlantic Ocean!"

It was shortly after receiving this startling information, and after Doc had absented himself from headquarters for several hours, that the bronze man made his announcement.

"The mystery will be solved in Europe," he had said surprisingly.

"But how?" Ham had asked. And then his eyes brightened. "You mean, Doc, because that millionaire, Duval, went there?"

The bronze giant's reply was, at first, puzzling.

"Duval is involved in this thing," he said. "But he is not the villain we are after. And yet it will be necessary to proceed to Europe before we clean up everything."

The truth suddenly became clear to Long Tom, listening intently. He recalled pertinent questions that Doc Savage had asked him.

Long Tom suddenly realized that Doc Savage had the mystery figured out! He was planning this last, strategic move!

Doc accompanied the others as far as Ambrose Light, where he departed from the ocean liner along with the harbor pilot.

The bronze man had directed, "You will wait for me at the hotel in Paris which I have named—the one where Renny and Johnny are now stopping."

It was Monk who said, "You're gonna follow in the plane, Doc?"

Doc Savage nodded. "It will take our largest plane and all available space for necessary equipment," he said. "That's why the rest of you must go on this liner. Also, there is something to be attended to here."

Doc had told Ham and Long Tom something about what he intended doing before leaving for abroad. It seemed there was some sort of urgent appointment in Washington.

Doc departed, stating that he would meet the others in about four days in Paris.

Two days later, in New York, the bronze man heard the startling information.

There had been a mystery at sea. Newspapers were full of black headlines. Cable companies had been first to reveal the puzzling circumstance.

They had been unable to reach the *Sea Queen* with routine cablegrams. Other agencies reported similar trouble. Government departments verified the comments.

The *Sea Queen,* greatest liner afloat, apparently had disappeared from the high seas. It was impossible to contact the famous vessel. Neither had any word been received from her in the past twenty-four hours.

The *Sea Queen* was the liner on which Monk, Ham, Long Tom and the others had taken passage!

Within two hours after learning about the mystery of the *Sea Queen,* Doc Savage was in the great tri-motored, streamlined plane, headed out over the Atlantic.

Most of the special equipment had already been stored aboard the plane, and the bronze man had spent nearly all of those two hours in making a double check on the news reports of the liner's strange silence.

For almost half an hour, he talked on the telephone with certain navy officials in Washington. Whatever he learned appeared to throw no light on the mystery of the ocean liner.

Because when the bronze man started his long flight, his metallic features were grimly taut.

Sometime during that night, midway in the Atlantic, and flying at tremendous speed, Doc Savage heard the first of the S O S messages.

He made notations of the S O S calls each time they came through the ether. They probably lasted for well over an hour, and in the meantime, the bronze giant's ship had covered hundreds of miles.

All attempts by Doc to get in touch with the *Sea Queen* were useless. There were no replies to his urgent queries.

At four a.m., the S O S signals stopped, and there was complete silence after that. The bronze man's eyes held a question as his great plane droned on throughout the long night.

Using the automatic pilot, Doc Savage was able to take short naps. He showed little signs of fatigue, and this was perhaps explained by his remarkable physique, the constant and rigid training which he followed to keep himself in condition.

Late that afternoon, Doc circled the huge plane over famous Le Bourget Field. He had already radioed a message ahead to have Renny and Johnny meet him here at the airfield.

The bronze man set the plane down as though it might have been a light glider. The first to rush up to the plane when it rolled to a stop were the two aides.

One of the two was a giant of a fellow; the other tall and gaunt and looking like the advance agent for a funeral.

The giant-size one was Colonel John Renwick—better known as Renny—an engineer of repute.

The other man was William Harper Littlejohn. Everyone called him Johnny. He was as thin as a straw and wore glasses that contained thick lenses. He was perhaps one of the world's greatest archaeologists.

Renny boomed. "Doc! Didn't think you'd make it so quick. We just arrived here in time!"

The big engineer never talked in anything less than a bull roar. He and gaunt-looking Johnny were in the cabin doorway the moment the bronze man swung it open.

Sightseers had come running up, pushing close to the mammoth ship.

The gaunt archaeologist, Johnny, paused in the cabin doorway, stared at the crowd and said studiously, "Illustrate some manifestation of migration!"

The Frenchman grouped about, stared.

"He means," Renny boomed, "scram! *Allez! Vite!*

Renny's lionlike roar made the crowd withdraw.

Johnny was inside the plane, his face very sober.

"Doc!" he said. "We heard about that liner—the one you said Ham, Monk and the others were coming across on! Do you think they—"

Johnny let the words trail off, but what he meant was significant. The archaeologist forgot to use big words whenever he talked with Doc Savage.

Renny added: "Doc, do you think they . . . they're really lost at sea, I mean—dead?"

Renny's gloomy look was sadder than ever.

Before replying, the bronze man led the two aides to the cockpit of the plane, indicated a chart which he had used on the ocean hop. At various points on the chart, there were notations and marks. Strung out in a line, each mark was connected by straight lines to a single circle at some point distant.

Doc Savage said quietly, "The marks indicate bearings taken on the S O S calls from the *Sea Queen*."

Renny nodded quickly. "Sure, the papers here were full of it. And then those S O S calls finally stopped, didn't they, Doc?"

The bronze man agreed. "But," he went on, "by taking the readings from the plane, flying at hundreds of miles per hour, it was possible to get angles and to figure distance to the source of those messages. They were faked."

Both aides stared. "Faked?"

Doc Savage indicated, with his finger, the single circle on the chart to which all the straight lines ran.

"The S O S signals from the *Sea Queen* came from that point," he said. "And that circle indicates a small island two hundred miles off the coast of France, in the Atlantic."

Later, Doc Savage turned plane and equipment over to the care of the two aides. At the airport, arrangements were made for the bronze man to use a fast, smaller ship, which he leased from one of the local airlines.

First, however, the bronze man sent Renny and Johnny on a quest for some special devices that he wanted to use in the rented plane.

Doc managed to get an hour of rest before setting out at dawn for the island off the seacoast. As he explained to the two aides:

"Stand ready to hear from me at your hotel. Also, one of you might check on all plane arrivals here and at other airports. Learn what you can about a man named Birmingham Jones."

Doc described Birmingham Jones in detail. "It is important that we find him."

Renny frowned. "But in your last message from New York, you said that the man behind this thing was called Valentine."

The bronze man nodded. "True. But Valentine, the real villain, has not yet revealed himself. He is working through this front, this Birmingham Jones."

Doc then added a detail that seemed to have no bearing on a man named Valentine. He mentioned the names of two countries that were at war, at the moment, in Europe. He said:

"You might check closely on any new developments in the situation between those two countries. Our embassy here will perhaps cooperate."

Soon, Doc Savage was putting the small, fast ship in the air. He took off as smoothly as though he had been flying the strange plane all his life.

And an hour later, the sun was getting warm in the sky when he picked out the hazy outline of the island far out to sea.

Moments later, Doc Savage was circling the isolated bit of land.

The size of the island would be, apparently, about four miles long and two wide. Hills rose up steeply from the rocky shore line at the southern end of the place. To the north, in what must have been a deep bay, the liner was tied up.

Doc dropped down lower in order to get a better view of the wooded isle.

The shrill, whistling whine came so abruptly that Doc Savage only had an instant's glimpse of the thing plunging upward through the slight ground haze.

Then there was the burst of smoke from the bronze man's plane and he was abruptly tumbling in the crazy spiral toward the southern tip of the island.

The smoke enveloped the entire plane, forming a black ball, and within that dark core the plane motor sputtered and choked and then roared.

Swaying back anf forth crazily, the plane continued its wild plunge toward the bit of land.

Chapter XV

RESCUE

Somewhere near the southern tip of the island, from atop a wooded hill, a tattered-looking group of men watched the plunge of the bronze man's plane.

Those who stared skyward, their eyes wide, were Ham, Monk, Long Tom, and the girl—Honey Sanders —and her red-headed boy friend, Tod Smith.

Their clothing was torn and ragged, a result of pushing through the thick undergrowth that was almost everywhere, Monk's already homely face was scratched and blood-flecked. He looked like an ape with measles.

Even Ham's dapper attire was half in shreds. His appearance looked incongruous when compared to the slender, polished black cane that he was carrying. The cane was one that had been returned to Doc's headquarters from the damaged car left near Sleepy Hollow. Ham had brought the sword-cane with him on the voyage.

Ham, watching as the falling plane vanished beyond the crest of a hill to the south, let out a moan.

"I have a hunch," he said tensely.

Monk gave his partner a dirty look. "Hunch about what, shyster?" he demanded.

"That Doc might have been in that ship!"

Everyone stared. It was the girl, Honey, who looked thoughtfully at Ham. She came over to his side, making a hopeless attempt to fold her torn skirt around her shapely, slender legs.

"Why do you say that?" Honey asked. Sunlight touched her soft golden hair, and she was beautiful.

"Because," said Ham, "they released one of those flying things from the liner, and brought the plane down. It must have been Doc!"

Monk started jumping up and down. "Blast their hides!" he piped shrilly. "How're we gonna get back on that ship in order to get at 'em?"

Young Tod Smith spoke up. "With machine guns trained on us from the decks, how do you *expect* to get back?" he demanded.

Monk scratched his head. "Must be some way!" he insisted.

They were interrupted by a crashing through the underbrush near the clearing in which they stood. All recognized the girl's self-appointed bodyguard—Sandy Gower.

The round-looking little constable's green tweed suit was almost in ribbons. His flame-orange necktie looked like lengths of shoestrings tied around his neck. But his pipe was still stuck in his mouth.

Panting, he came running up to the group. "Why didn't you wait for me?" he demanded breathlessly. "Gosh!"

Monk said sourly, "Some cop!" And then, "Brother, we were lookin' out for ourselves!"

The girl asked, "Sandy, how did you manage to escape?"

Sandy Gower gasped, "Heard those crooks talking —I was hiding down in one of the cargo holds—and they said something about you jumping overboard and escaping here in the woods. I tried the same."

The stocky constable indicated a blood-red crease across his right arm. "They saw me—and almost winged me with one of them machine guns they got on deck! Whew!"

Long Tom had been saying nothing. He appeared to be listening intently, his pale eyes unusually bright. His sudden announcement drew the others up alert.

"You know," Long Tom said sharply, "I don't think that plane crashed. I'm gonna take a look!"

The skinny electrical wizard started toward the crest of the wooded hill. The others plunged through the tangle of junglelike growth, behind him.

A little later they managed to force their way down the far side of the hill; reached, finally, a strip of beach that was the southern tip of the island.

Doc Savage was just climbing out of the plane that had been landed there.

For moments, everyone except the bronze man was talking at once. Then, finally, Doc made brief explanations.

"Renny and Johnny obtained the smoke-screen chemical for the plane exhaust. It was quite possible, after the liner's location had been learned, that they would try to ward off any approach to the vessel."

Doc's aides immediately understood. The bronze man, avoiding the flying death that had been released from the liner, had wrapped the diving plane in a chemical smoke screen to give the idea that it had caught fire and crashed.

Doc said, "It is quite clear that Valentine's gang took over the liner at sea?" The sentence was both a question and statement of fact.

Ham nodded. "They've got the crew in their power," the lawyer explained. "There weren't many passengers, as you recall, and nearly all of them are Valentine's henchmen. Some of the others went to Europe on those Clipper planes."

Monk added, "Yeah. And, Doc, they got a couple of big-shot European army guys that were sailing too. They're holding those army experts for somethin'!"

Doc appeared to be interested in the remark. He said, "Renny will be trying to contact us soon. Is the radio aboard the liner in working order?"

"Sure!" Monk exclaimed. "But what the heck, Doc? How you gonna *use* it? Those birds have machine guns on deck, and plenty of ammunition. We ain't got a chance!"

Doc had suddenly stepped to the nearby small plane. He returned quickly with several of his machine pistols. He passed these to his three aides, who had been relieved of any weapons while aboard the liner at sea.

Doc said quickly, "There is only room for one extra with me in the plane. Ham will be that passenger. The rest of you return to the liner—but stay well clear of it for at least half an hour. You should be able to board it then."

Ruddy-faced Sandy Gower stared. "But how—" he started.

Doc and Ham were already headed back to the plane. A moment later the bronze man took off and put the fast little ship swiftly into the sky.

Doc flew low, so that he could not be seen by anyone at the northern part of the island, where he had observed the ocean liner tied up in the bay.

Even Ham was puzzled. Seated beside the bronze giant in the plane's small cockpit, he asked, "How do you expect to ever get aboard that boat, Doc?"

Doc Savage indicated a drum of some kind of chemical that was in the cockpit. A connecting, tubular line ran from the drum to the hookup with the engine exhaust.

"When we drop down over the liner," Doc directed, "open the petcock on that drum."

A moment later, the liner leaped into sight beyond the trees. Doc was putting the fast-moving ship down in a low, flat plunge, and shortly they were close over the ship.

As Ham turned the petcock on the drum of fluid, a thick, whitish smoke poured out behind the plane. Heavier than air, it dropped like a huge blanket, to slowly envelop the massive vessel tied up below.

Smoke coming from the ship's funnels indicated that it had been about ready to leave the island.

Doc turned the plane around, came back above the whitish screen that was flattening out below. He directed Ham to lay down more of the peculiar smoky stuff.

As Doc explained, "Form of anæsthetic gas. Drawn in through the vessel's ventilators, it should knock everyone out in a matter of moments. It will dissipate rapidly."

After that, they kept flying around for about fifteen minutes. The whitish smoke screen had slowly cleared. Again the liner was visible below them as they flew close.

Men lay sprawled on her decks. There appeared to be no sign of life aboard whatsoever.

Doc Savage set the plane down in a clearing near the bay, and shortly he and Ham were approaching the huge liner.

At sometime in the past, the northern end of the island around the bay must have been inhabited. There were some tumble-down fishing shacks and sagging wharfs. In deep water, the liner had been anchored nearby, out in the bay.

Doc and Ham found a leaky old rowboat and got out to the vessel. The only way of getting aboard the towering liner was by climbing the chain leading up from her anchor.

A strange sight met their eyes on the upper decks.

The crooks who had taken over the boat were piled around like flies. They all appeared to be sleeping. The members of the crew were found in similar attitudes.

And below decks, in cabins and staterooms and through every part of the great ship, more sleeping people were found.

Monk and the others arrived while Doc was making the inspection. As Doc commented, "The effects of the anæsthetic gas will keep them like this several more hours. We will have to hurry."

"What are you gonna do with this mob?" Monk asked. "I mean, all those that belong to Birmingham's crowd?"

Doc directed, "Swing out one of the largest lifeboats. Sandy Gower and young Tod Smith can help."

In the next quarter of an hour, the bronze man's plan became evident.

First, he located all officers of the liner. The skipper was found, also unconscious, tied up in his stateroom near the bridge.

Doc used a hypodermic needle and a stimulant taken from his equipment vest. Shortly he had all the officers awake and on their feet.

It was only natural that, recognizing Doc Savage, they immediately pitched in to help.

It appeared that there had been one of Birmingham Jones' thugs for every officer aboard the ship. This went for the crew, also. Practically the entire passenger list had been composed of crooks employed by the wily Birmingham Jones.

Thus, movement of the liner had been completely in the crooks' hands.

But now they were lowered in the lifeboat, taken ashore, and laid out like a long line of corpses on one of the old piers. The job took two or three hours, and Doc Savage urged haste.

Birmingham Jones, along with scar-faced Pinky, was located in one of the best suites aboard. They, too, were unconscious, having breathed of the gassed air coming through the efficient ventilating system!

But the bronze man did not put Birmingham Jones and Pinky ashore with the others. He gave them each a treatment with the hypo needle.

Awake, seeing the situation, realizing the efficiency of this remarkable bronze fellow, Birmingham Jones suddenly decided that perhaps he had been working for the wrong crowd.

"Got an idea," he suggested, in his smooth manner.

Monk looked over the tall, well-dressed Birmingham carefully.

"Yeah," he remarked. "You got some swell ideas. Like killing people, maybe!"

But Birmingham Jones shook his dark head. "Look," he said, "you think I'm kidding, don't you?"

"You guessed it!" rapped Monk.

"Well, I'll show you. I'll take you to that Valentine fella."

Pinky offered to pitch in with Doc's crowd, too.

Doc Savage was listening quietly. You know where Patrick Valentine is?" Doc put in.

Birmingham Jones nodded. "He's got most of those flying things at a base near the Swiss border. He's planning, right at this moment, the grandest wholesale murder you ever heard of, partner!"

"And the others—some of those who went on the Clipper planes?" Doc prodded.

"We were aboard one of them ships," Birmingham said. "But we changed over to the liner. The other guys are already at Valentine's base there near Switzerland."

The bronze man said, "Perhaps we can check on that," and disappeared in the direction of the liner's radio room.

He was gone for some time. In the meantime, the remainder of the crooks aboard ship—all the unconscious ones—were put ashore on the isolated, small island.

Doc returned. "Renny and Johnny have been doing some checking up," he announced. "What Birmingham Jones says is correct. We will pick up Renny and Johnny at this place Birmingham has mentioned."

Just before Doc gave orders to pull up the anchor, Sandy Gower exclaimed worriedly, "You going to let those fellows on the island starve, Doc Savage? After

all, it might be some time before you get back here to
pick them up!"

The bronze man explained quietly, "Cases of beans
and hardtack have been left for them. Also water."

A moment later, under the skipper's close eye, the
great vessel eased out of the harbor and headed toward
France.

Chapter XVI

BREAKNECK PASS

Two persons aboard ship seemed especially interested in that short voyage to the mainland.

One of the two was well-dressed, tall Birmingham
Jones; the other, the crook with the battered features
—Pinky.

Birmingham Jones had been assigned a cabin aboard
the liner. And it was Pinky who, acting furtively, had
slipped into Birmingham's room and locked the door
behind him.

Pinky grinned, commented, "You sure fooled that
Doc Savage crowd, brother. Nice going!"

Birmingham Jones was seated in a chair and polishing his fingernails. An automatic lay within reach on a
table beside him.

"I *guess* so," he remarked absently. Then, "What do
you want? Thought I told you to be careful?"

Pinky's scarred features sobered. "Look," he said.
"What did Doc Savage want with you and that slick-
looking gent named Ham? Saw the three of you headed
up to the bridge a while ago."

Birmingham Jones continued polishing his nails.

"They were talking to that fella they called Renny.
Using the radio."

The smartly dressed Birmingham abruptly frowned. The sort of vacant stare that frequently came into his pale eyes, was there now.

"Say," he asked, "I almost forgot the name of that place where Valentine said to send Doc and his bunch. Hope I got it right. What was it again?"

Pinky shook his head, sighed wearily.

"Lookit," he said grimly. "They call it Breakneck Pass." He mentioned the name of a small village near the Swiss border, in the foothills of the Alps. "I hope you got it right."

Birmingham Jones nodded. "I got it right. I remember it now."

Pinky looked relieved. "You sure act foggy sometimes, Birmingham!"

Birmingham Jones picked up the automatic. "Who's foggy?" he demanded quietly.

Pinky jumped.

"All right! All right!" he said soothingly. "Skip it. But—"

"But what?"

"You sure you told them where to go there near the base of that Breakneck pass—to the place where Valentine has the trap all set for them?"

Birmingham nodded confidently. "Hell, yes! This time tomorrow, Doc Savage and his crowd will be blown to hell and gone!"

Pinky grinned. "Valentine sure fooled that bunch, didn't he?"

"Yeah."

Birmingham Jones abruptly indicated the door. "Now scram!" he rapped. "I gotta see Doc Savage in a few minutes. We'll be docking in a little while. You stay with them and pretend to be ready with any information they want."

Pinky nodded and went out. On the deck where Doc Savage and the others had staterooms, he found that something was apparently wrong. One of the bronze man's aides was creating a lot of noise.

It was hairy Monk, and the chemist was yelling

worriedly, "He's gone. Looked over the whole danged ship for him—an' he's gone!"

Everyone was grouped around Monk. There was the bronze man and skinny Long Tom, and with them the girl and her boy friend Tod Smith.

Frowning, stocky little Sandy Gower pushed his red face into the group circled about the hairy chemist.

"Who's gone?" Sandy Gower demanded. Back on the ship again, he had obtained a change of clothing. His newest suit and necktie were even more atrocious-looking than those he had worn previously.

Monk squalled, "Ham's gone, that's who!"

"Ham's gone where?" Sandy Gower prodded.

It was Doc Savage who spoke up quietly:

"It appears," he said, "that Ham Brooks has vanished from this boat."

And Ham was still missing when the liner finally docked and everyone had been put aboard the boat train for Paris.

Every part of the great ship had been searched. Monk even went down into the holds and through the very bilges of the ship. He had returned appearing as though he had crawled through sewers.

But no trace had been found of the lawyer, Ham.

To Monk's dismay, Doc Savage said they would have to go on without Ham. There was little time to lose Some of the others could not understand the bronze man's attitude. But no one questioned Doc Savage's verdict.

In Paris, Doc Savage did another strange thing. He did not try to contact his other two aides, Renny and Johnny Littlejohn. Instead, the bronze man made arrangements for the rental of two large touring cars.

Monk, puzzled, asked, "Why aren't we taking them with us, Doc? Thought you left a whole lot of our equipment with them in the big plane you flew to France?"

The bronze man nodded. "The equipment has already been moved to that location which Birmingham

Jones has given us. We will get in touch with Renny and Johnny later."

And later, riding in the big touring cars through the night, on the fast trip toward the Swiss frontier, it was scar-faced Pinky who managed to get a chance to whisper to Birmingham Jones.

"Sweet hell!" Pinky said. "This is gonna be good! We even got that bronze man's stuff placed where Valentine can wipe it out along with Doc Savage's crowd!"

Birmingham Jones nodded. His pale eyes were bleak and cold.

Sometime early that morning, the cars crawled slowly up into the foothills. Pretty Honey Sanders and the others had managed to take cat naps throughout the night. But Doc, Long Tom and Monk had taken turns driving during the long hours before dawn. These amazing worldwide adventurers never seemed to tire.

In the last village, they had picked up papers. Monk managed to get one that was printed in English, and seated beside Doc Savage—who was at the wheel of the first car—Monk was reading headlines.

"It says here," the chemist exclaimed, "that those two nations that are havin' a war are sure raisin' plenty of hell!"

From the rear seat, Honey Sanders said, "It's terrible. All Europe will be involved shortly!"

Sandy Gower was seated with the girl. Young Tod Smith was riding in the trailing car, with Pinky, Birmingham Jones and Long Tom.

The constable put in, "War ought to be stopped. It ain't right to have wars."

Quietly, the bronze man commented, "It looks like this war will be over shortly—if thousands of men continue to be killed wantonly as they have been in the past few days."

Monk had been reading some more.

"Yeah, Doc," he commented. "Says here that one of them countries has a secret kind of gun that is wiping the other nation's men out like ants!"

"Did you read all of that article?" Doc prodded.

Monk read, and shortly he frowned.

"Say!" he piped. "It says here that both those danged countries are accusing the other of having a secret war machine."

"Exactly," added Doc Savage, and there was something about the bronze man's tone that caused Monk to stare at him questioningly.

Usually, the hairy chemist could appear pretty dumb. And yet, for all his homely looks and crazy actions, Monk had a good brain. Frequently, the chemist's acts were merely put on to get Ham's goat.

But now there was a mystery concerning Ham's disappearance, and Monk was worried. Oddly, these two strange fellows thought a lot of each other—despite the fact that they always seemed ready to murder one another when together.

Monk was thinking about what the bronze man had just said, and was making no comments. He sat with his chin in his big hand, his brow wrinkled.

Doc Savage drove in silence, and the road got narrower and steeper. It was getting cold. Rising up like grim, sky-reaching sentinels around them, were the peaks of the Alps, snow visible seemingly only a few hundred feet above.

Doc had been following a route outlined by Birmingham when they had left the last village. But even small farmhouses were left behind now. The valley through which they had climbed grew slowly narrower, seemed to wall them in like the sides of a canyon that had no summit.

The road forked, and Doc Savage took the right turn-off. He forced the car ahead for several more miles—when abruptly those in this first machine heard the others yelling at them from behind.

Doc stopped.

Tod Smith, Birmingham Jones and Pinky came running up to them. Long Tom remained at the wheel of the second car.

Birmingham Jones exclaimed, "Pinky, here, just reminded me that we took the wrong turn-off. Should have followed that other road back there!"

But Doc Savage made no attempt to turn the car around. Instead, he said, "It is quite possible this road will meet the other again."

Pinky frowned. "But if we're gonna get to that Breakneck Pass hide-out—" he started.

"We will continue on this road," stated the bronze man quietly.

Everyone was puzzled by the bronze man's actions, but they continued.

A half mile farther on, where the route passed directly beneath sheer cliffs that poked up on either side of them, the sound like distant thunder suddenly reached their ears.

Doc drew the car up, stared toward the snow-covered mountainsides.

The others stared, too, toward a point not more than a quarter of a mile behind them. They saw the phenomenon that appeared like a white Niagara plunging down directly over the narrow roadway.

Monk let out a howl. "We're trapped!" he piped shrilly. "Lookit, will ya? Avalanche!"

And the avalanche came down and made a small white mountain on that part of the road which they had, a moment before, passed over.

Chapter XVII

DEATH TORPEDO

Everyone stood there, staring as the snow piled up like a glacier behind them, down the narrow road, and it was scar-faced Pinky who started yelling.

"Whatta we gonna do?" he demanded. "This is the

wrong road, and now we won't get to that Valentine hide-out."

Doc Savage ordered, "Back into the cars. We will continue just the same."

No one saw the worried glance that flashed from Pinky to Birmingham Jones. The glance practically said, "Something's got to be done! Savage has pulled a fast one on us!"

But with the road blocked behind them, there was nothing that the two could do about it—if Birmingham was planning a double cross.

They drove another hour, and abruptly the route—surprisingly—fell away from the encircling mountains and they were at the approach to a wide, endless-looking plateau. Also, they had come to the junction of another road.

Doc Savage stopped the cars and said, "We have arrived at Breakneck Pass from an opposite direction."

All followed his indicating hand.

Off to the left, a short way back from the road which they had just intercepted, rose the straight, steep walls of a cut through the mountains. From where they stood, it appeared impossible that a road could ever find its way through such a narrow space.

Everyone was standing, looking at what Doc Savage indicated.

At the bronze man's next words, various things suddenly happened with amazing speed.

Doc said: "It was a clever way to lead us to death. But now we will take them by surprise, by coming into the Pass from this opposite direction."

Tough-looking Pinky suddenly had a gun in his fists. He was backing toward one of the emptied cars.

"Not *me!*" Pinky rapped. "Stand back—everybody!" He kept them covered with the gun, clipped out an order.

"C'mon, Birmingham! *We're* getting the hell outta here!"

Nattily dressed Birmingham Jones leaped after his partner. As did stocky Sandy Gower, the girl's self-appointed bodyguard.

"Me, too!" Sandy Gower yelled worriedly. "I'm getting *outta* here!"

Under cover of Pinky's menacing gun, the other two piled into the big car. Birmingham Jones drove, wheeling the car around recklessly in the roadway.

Monk howled, "Doc! You gonna let them get away with that?"

Oddly, the bronze man had not moved.

Now he said swiftly, "Let them go."

Monk and Long Tom were all for leaping in the other car and following, but at the bronze man's command they hesitated.

Young, red-haired Tom Smith was puzzled, too. He said, "I've never trusted those other two, but I thought Sandy Gower had some guts!"

The car was already rocketing down the road, toward the long plateau that stretched out endlessly in the opposite direction.

Doc Savage whipped into sudden action then. He jumped behind the wheel of the second car, ordered the others inside. Then he was sending the car down the road, not after the men who had ran out on them—but into Breakneck Pass.

Monk piped worriedly, "Blazes, Doc! You're running right into that trap Valentine has set for us. That Birmingham was kidding us all the time!"

Skinny Long Tom added: "Yeah, Doc, maybe you've made a mistake!"

"There's no mistake," announced the bronze man grimly, and he kept driving.

The road narrowed, started into the crevice between the sheer rock walls of Breakneck Pass.

The men stepped out ahead of them and started firing at the car.

Doc's swift order sent everyone piling out of the machine the moment he had flung it around so that it rested crosswise in the road. Doc and the others were momentarily protected on the far side of the big car.

Long Tom and Monk were quickly using the machine pistols. The weapons sent bullfiddle roars shivering up and down the canyon walls. Men some distance beyond the other side of the blocking car started falling down.

But their injuries would not be permanent. For the special guns that Doc's aides used were firing a form of "mercy" bullet of Doc's own invention. The bullets, aimed at the attackers' legs, inflicted only temporary paralysis.

But more men came out of the Pass, along the narrow roadway, and opened up fire with guns that contained real slugs.

Abruptly, from high overhead, came a roar as something came swooping down out of the sky, to flatten out and zoom overhead where the canyon walls widened out high above.

Monk howled with fear. "The flying *thing!*" he started to say. "We're gonna be blasted to hell an'—"

But above Monk's outburst, Doc said quietly, "That should be Renny and Johnny in the plane."

Monk, crouched down behind the car, stared upward, squinting.

And he saw Doc's trimotored, streamlined ship—the one that the bronze man had left at the Paris airport.

Monk started jumping up and down and waving his arms at the plane. A slug whined by his head.

Long Tom reached up and yanked the excited chemist down beside the others. "You want to get killed, you dunce!" the electrical wizard snorted.

Doc Savage said, "Hold your fire. Watch!"

The big plane came down so low between the canyon walls that it seemed a certainty the ship's wings would be ripped asunder against the rock walls.

But they cleared, and then the sound like the rattle of a machine gun reached the ears of those with Doc Savage. Something like rain spattered the dust in the roadway ahead. The pellets also hit the small mob of attackers crouched there, and they started lying down on their stomachs and dropping their weapons.

They didn't get up again. No reinforcements joined them.

The trimotored ship zoomed skyward, circled when it was safely clear of the Pass, and disappeared.

Doc Savage said, "It is safe to proceed now."

Pretty Honey Sanders stared at the unconscious assailants piled up in the roadway just ahead. She looked at Doc Savage. She was beginning to understand some of the remarkable ingenuity of this big bronze fellow.

The girl said, "You knew about this trap all the time, didn't you? You had plans made for those two you call Renny and Johnny to meet you here?"

Doc said quietly, "Renny had orders to pick up our trail into the mountains today. He has been flying above us for the past hour, high enough so that the plane was not heard by anyone in the cars."

Young Tod Smith gave Doc Savage a steady regard. He, too, had been puzzled by some of the bronze giant's apparently questionable movements. Now he understood.

Monk was all for going ahead and waking up some of the sleeping thugs and bashing in a few heads.

But Doc rapped, "Hurry! It will only be a matter of moments now!"

"Moments until what?" Long Tom wanted to know.

But the bronze man did not explain. Instead, he led the way along the road. They saw that it curved sharply, right in the heart of the mountain pass. Beyond, where a little clump of woods grew in close between steep walls and roadway, Doc pointed and said, "It should be in there."

Monk and Long Tom were still puzzled. "What is it?" Monk asked.

Doc did not answer. Instead, he pushed into the enshrouding trees, with the others close behind him.

The girl's deep-blue eyes were wide with excitement. She exclaimed, "This is the best time I ever had *in my life*."

Tod Smith winced and commented, "Hope you get over it before many years!"

Doc said significantly, "What they have in store for us yet will not be very pleasant!"

And as if to lend emphasis to the statement, the high, shrill whining sound came down off the canyon walls. It became a sharp screech that almost pierced the eardrums.

Monk started to say, "Betcha that's Renny and Johnny again—"

And then he let out a howl and stared.

The flying thing was high enough that a clear view of it was vague. And yet the hairy chemist saw enough of it to be apparently sure of his deductions.

"Doc!" he squalled. "It's that flying hobgoblin of a thing from Sleepy Hollow. One of them blasted things that wrecked the schooner and—"

"Yes," said Doc Savage. "It is the aërial torpedo."

"What—" the girl started to ask.

Before Doc could reply, the thing that flew with the speed of a comet had passed far overhead. A split second later, there came the terrific blast. For a moment, it felt as if the mountains would shatter all around them.

Doc ripped out, "They'll have the range shortly. Help me with this thing."

Doc had reached what looked like an old, long farm wagon loaded with strange-looking scientific apparatus. With Monk's and Long Tom's aid, he quickly pushed the strange unit onto the roadway.

Instantly, Doc Savage was up in the big wagon, manipulating gadgets that were on the heavy instrument-cases and equipment.

Long Tom seemed to gather immediately what the equipment was for, because he leaped to assist the bronze man.

Shortly, everyone heard the hum of powerful radio tubes.

Doc whipped a covering from one particularly large case. Compact storage batteries were revealed. The bronze man, his metallic fingers moving with skilled speed, was making various hook-ups.

Without pausing in his swift movements, he directed,

"Long Tom, the ray machine is covered up there at the other end of the wagon. Uncover it!"

The machine was the one Doc Savage had used back at his New York headquarters. Apparently he had brought it aboard in his big plane. Renny, though, had flown the equipment here.

Shortly, Doc had a short-wave transmitting set in readiness. Then he was speaking into a microphone:

"Ham?" he asked. "Is everyone clear of the aërial torpedoes?"

The others stared at Doc's mention of Ham.

A reply came back through a portable loud-speaker that had been hooked up. Ham said tensely:

"Yes, Doc. All except Valentine. I'm with Renny and Johnny in the plane. But, Doc—"

"Yes?"

"Valentine's releasing those things. You'd better clear out! Valentine managed to elude us the moment we got here, and he's in his place now—alone!"

"Then stay clear," finished the bronze man, and cut Ham off.

Monk, wide-eyed, piped, "I don't get this, Doc? Where the blazes is that shyster—"

But Doc Savage was manipulating another set of radio-control dials. His face was tense, his flake-gold eyes revealing that his brain was working furiously.

He started to say, "If we can pick up the range of the next one—"

The screaming, high-pitched sound came down out of the sky again—and this time the flying thing of death was very close.

It was so close over their heads that there was a peculiar burned-ozone smell in the air.

Chapter XVIII

FAREWELL TO DEATH

So close that they saw the long, cylindricallike object. Those with Doc Savage stared at the hurtling torpedo as it ripped through the mountain pass. It could not have been more than a hundred feet above their heads. The thing appeared to have fins, and a taillike structure.

It did not explode, but disappeared swiftly.

Long Tom was frantically adjusting the ray machine, directing the machine after the flying object that had already disappeared.

"Too late," commented Doc, from where he was at the radio controls. "Wait!"

His fingers moved deftly. Various delicate instruments that he watched closely seemed to tell the bronze man some fact.

For he said to the skinny electrical wizard, "If this doesn't work, then we are done for!"

He pressed a small button on the radio-control set.

Somewhere—it was impossible to tell the distance—there was a violent blast, as though tons of dynamite might have been set off somewhere out of their sight.

The bronze man's unusual eyes flickered. Not taking his hands from the radio dials, he said, "Monk, hurry back and get the car."

Monk was gone about ten minutes. Upon his return with the big touring car, he said, "Had to move some of them sleeping mugs outta the way, or run over them!"

Abruptly there was a crackling in the loud-speaker unit which Doc Savage had set up. Into the microphone, he said, "Yes?"

"Doc?" It was Renny's booming voice this time, obviously coming from the plane that was flying at some point distant.

"What is it?" prodded Doc Savage.

"You all right?"

The bronze man assured Renny that they were all still alive. He told briefly of the aërial torpedo appearance, added, "It looks like we have just brought the last one down. At least, the thing exploded a moment ago."

Renny's voice got worried. *"Listen, Doc, Valentine's gone completely nuts. We can't get at him, because of the danger of one of those things hitting the plane. But he's ready to release more of them!"*

"We have figured on that," said the bronze man. "Stand by while we close in. What is the distance to Valentine's headquarters?"

"Exactly three miles," came Renny's answer.

Doc swung away from the transmitter, gave brief orders.

"Load this radio equipment in the rear of the car," he directed. "Fast!"

With the storage batteries that were needed for operation of the radio-control apparatus, the rear seat of the car was jammed. Long Tom, however, managed to squeeze his skinny frame in. Monk hung onto the running board while the girl and Tod Smith climbed in the front seat with the bronze man.

As Doc drove, he gave explicit directions to Long Tom.

The electrical wizard apparently understood Doc's purpose, for once he said, "Nothing yet, Doc."

Doc Savage sent the machine racing down the narrow road, back the way they had come. They passed the point where Monk had piled the unconscious assailants alongside the road. Later, they passed the junction where Sandy Gower, Birmingham Jones and Pinky had run out on them.

Two miles beyond this, where the roadway bordered the plateau of a place they had seen earlier, they saw the long, low metal building far out in a field.

Doc said, "That's it. That's the place Valentine's set up here in this isolated section."

High above them, circling like a lazy bird in the clear sky, was a plane. It was Doc's trimotored ship.

The girl suddenly cried, "Listen!"

But everyone had heard the sound.

It started as a low moan, and quickly seemed to get shriller and higher in tone.

Doc rasped out: "O. K., Long Tom. *Get it!*"

As Doc Savage had done a while ago, so did Long Tom depress a button on the radio-control set.

At the same moment, the building off in the flat field appeared to disintegrate. It went up in the air, and a terrific explosion followed.

The silence of the lonesome spot was shattered by the explosions that followed during the next fifteen minutes.

Doc held the car clear, and after waiting another fifteen minutes—after the explosions had stopped—he rolled the machine slowly down the road in the direction of what had once been a building.

Only a pile of debris now remained.

Renny set the big plane down in the field alongside them. He and gaunt Johnny Littlejohn, the archaeologist piled out and ran up to Doc and the others.

Birmingham Jones came running along behind them.

Monk stared. The girl's fingers flew to her mouth. Tod Smith and Long Tom looked quickly at the bronze man.

But Monk said, "Blazes, Doc! Thought that Birmingham Jones was with—"

The tall, nattily attired Birmingham Jones had reached the group. He looked at Monk and said coolly:

"Listen, ape, who ever gave you the right to think, anyway?"

Monk almost jumped out of his shoes.

"Ham!" he yelled.

Doc Savage explained, "Ham and Birmingham Jones were about the same height and build. It was only necessary for Ham to use the glass eyeshells to make his eyes look like Birmingham's."

Ham, grinning at bewildered Monk, was removing the paper-thin shells from his eyes. Transparent, the tiny objects were a product that could be bought in any high-class optical shop.

Honey Sanders exclaimed, "But if this was Ham all the time, then where is the *real* Birmingham Jones?"

Doc Savage said, "Birmingham Jones was put back on the island with the rest of the prisoners there. Ham was planted with the one named Pinky in order to learn Valentine's plans and the exact location of this aërial torpedo base."

All were staring at the demolished building. The biting odor of burned ozone was in the air.

Young Tod Smith asked, "You mean, Valentine was sending those torpedo things out from *there?*"

Doc nodded.

"But how—" Tod Smith started.

"Valentine," Doc went on, "was using a type of perpetual-motion machine employing an atomic or perhaps a molecular force. Once started, the torpedoes traveled faster and farther than any known speed ship. They were operated by remote radio control. They could be exploded in like manner, at any point where Valentine wished them to do so."

Tod Smith's eyes brightened. "I get it!" he said. "That's why you were using this remote-control radio set of your own! *You* set off the torpedo that Valentine was ready to launch!"

Doc said quietly, "Yes. It is too bad that Pinky had to die along with him, there in the building. But it was either that or perhaps death for thousands."

The girl, Honey, was staring.

"Pinky?" she gasped. "But *he* was with Sandy Gower. Where is Sandy Gower now?"

What was evident to the others, had been overlooked by the girl.

Doc moved across to where she was standing, said gently, "Sandy Gower *was* Valentine."

It was two days later, again aboard the liner, that Doc Savage and the others prepared to sail for the island where the rest of the prisoners would be picked up.

Newspapers, that morning, were full of headlines. Monk and Ham were commenting about them.

"See where those two countries that were fighting have signed a truce," Monk said. "Both of them figured the other had a new gun that was wiping out their troops by the thousands. Both decided to quit!"

Ham looked at the bronze man.

"And that was Valentine's—Sandy Gower's—idea, wasn't it Doc?" he asked.

Doc nodded.

"Sandy Gower had an idea that he was going to stop all wars. He became a fanatic on the idea, standing ready to kill thousands in order to accomplish his purpose. He perfected his aërial torpedo there in the schooner workshop near Sleepy Hollow. Then he was shipping them to that mountain hide-out over here."

Doc looked at pretty Honey Sanders. "You knew Sandy Gower. Inadvertently, you almost discovered that he was Valentine—though you did not realize it."

The girl was getting over her first shock at learning Sandy Gower had been the villain all along.

"I remember now," she explained, "how Sandy used to talk to dad by the hour about war, and that it should be stopped. Father was somewhat of a scientist, you know."

The bronze man nodded understandingly.

"But, Doc," Monk put in, "what about that rich guy, Duval? I figured he was mixed up in this thing? Where's he now?"

"Safely in New York," Doc said. "He never left the country. You see, Sandy Gower needed plenty of money to finance his crazy scheme. And so he sent Birmingham Jones to Duval, asking for that help. Naturally, Duval refused."

Monk shook his head quickly. "I get it. And so they used a little persuasion on Duval. Knocked down a couple of his shops with that flying Oscar thing, and made him kick through—or else!"

"That," Doc agreed, "was the general idea."

Renny had a word to say.

"We learned about that cathedral explosion in Paris, too," he offered. "Holy cow! It was caused by one of those torpedoes that Sandy Gower sent aboard. He shipped some of them that way, because the darned things could keep going almost forever. Only he miscalculated on that one, and it went through the cathedral!"

Ham's face was thoughtful. He looked at Doc Savage.

"Funny," he remarked, "about those two army men who were seized aboard this same ship by Birmingham Jones. We never did find those two men when we first searched this boat, Doc!"

Doc's face was just a trifle grim. "That," he said, "has been explained while we were after Sandy Gower."

"Explained?"

"A crew member," said Doc, "was too frightened to reveal it at first. He has now talked. The two army officials—after all war information had been extracted from them by Birmingham Jones—were murdered and dropped at sea. Birmingham Jones, when picked up at the island, will probably never be sent back to the college. He likes too well to kill people."

All understood what the bronze man meant.

Hairy Monk was abruptly staring around. He looked at Ham.

"Where's Honey?" he demanded, his eyes brightening hopefully.

Ham, strangely, looked somewhat downcast.

"Over there," he indicated, pointing.

Pretty Honey Sanders was over at the ship's rail, standing close to Tod Smith. The red-haired young man's arm was around the girl's shoulders. Her golden-rich hair brushed his cheek.

"That," said Ham, "let's *you* out, ape!"

Monk grinned at his dapper partner. "At least," he piped, "neither of us have a chance, so I ain't gonna feel so bad!"

To the world at large, Doc Savage is a strange, mysterious figure of glistening bronze skin and golden eyes. To his fans he is the greatest adventure hero of all time, whose fantastic exploits are unequaled for hair-raising thrills, breathtaking escapes, blood-curdling excitement!

☐	THE MOUNTAIN MONSTER	2239	$1.25
☐	THE MAN OF BRONZE	6352	$1.25
☐	THE BOSS OF TERROR	6424	$1.25
☐	THE THOUSAND HEADED MAN	6471	$1.25
☐	THE RED TERRORS	6486	$1.25
☐	DOC SAVAGE: HIS APOCALYPTIC LIFE	8834	$1.25
☐	THE KING MAKER	10042	$1.25
☐	THE SPOTTED MEN	10075	$1.25
☐	THE PHANTOM CITY	10119	$1.25
☐	THE MYSTIC MULLAH	10120	$1.25
☐	FEAR CAY	10121	$1.25
☐	LAND OF ALWAYS NIGHT	10122	$1.25
☐	FANTASTIC ISLAND	10125	$1.25
☐	QUEST OF QUI	10126	$1.25

Buy them at your local bookstore or use this handy coupon for ordering:

Bantam Book Catalog

Here's your up-to-the-minute listing of every book currently available from Bantam.

This easy-to-use catalog is divided into categories and contains over 1400 titles by your favorite authors.

So don't delay—take advantage of this special opportunity to increase your reading pleasure.

Just send us your name and address and 25¢ (to help defray postage and handling costs).